P9-APH-859

# A Dog Howled in the Distance.

William heard a musket shot.

They are after me already, he thought. He forced himself to his feet.

"I will find the monster!" a man shouted, his voice harsh with anger.

Close. Much too close.

Run, William urged himself. Run. You must survive. You must kill Catherine Hatchett. You must stop her evil. Do not let her beat you.

But two men stepped out to block his path.

"William Parker!" one of them shouted. "You cannot escape. You will hang from the tallest tree!"

## Books by R. L. Stine

*Fear Street*
THE NEW GIRL
THE SURPRISE PARTY
THE OVERNIGHT
MISSING
THE WRONG NUMBER
THE SLEEPWALKER
HAUNTED
HALLOWEEN PARTY
THE STEPSISTER
SKI WEEKEND
THE FIRE GAME
LIGHTS OUT
THE SECRET BEDROOM
THE KNIFE
PROM QUEEN
FIRST DATE
THE BEST FRIEND
THE CHEATER
SUNBURN
THE NEW BOY
THE DARE
BAD DREAMS
DOUBLE DATE
THE THRILL CLUB
ONE EVIL SUMMER
THE MIND READER
WRONG NUMBER 2
TRUTH OR DARE
DEAD END
FINAL GRADE
SWITCHED
COLLEGE WEEKEND

*Fear Street Super Chiller*
PARTY SUMMER
SILENT NIGHT
GOODNIGHT KISS
BROKEN HEARTS
SILENT NIGHT 2
THE DEAD LIFEGUARD
CHEERLEADERS: THE NEW EVIL
BAD MOONLIGHT

*The Fear Street Saga*
THE BETRAYAL
THE SECRET
THE BURNING

*Fear Street Cheerleaders*
THE FIRST EVIL
THE SECOND EVIL
THE THIRD EVIL

*99 Fear Street: The House of Evil*
THE FIRST HORROR
THE SECOND HORROR
THE THIRD HORROR

*The Cataluna Chronicles*
THE EVIL MOON
THE DARK SECRET

*Other Novels*
HOW I BROKE UP WITH ERNIE
PHONE CALLS
CURTAINS
BROKEN DATE

Available from ARCHWAY Paperbacks

For orders other than by individual consumers, Archway Books grants a discount on the purchase of **10 or more** copies of single titles for special markets or premium use. For further details, please write to the Vice-President of Special Markets, Pocket Books, 1230 Avenue of the Americas, New York, NY 10020.

For information on how individual consumers can place orders, please write to Mail Order Department, Paramount Publishing, 200 Old Tappan Road, Old Tappan, NJ 07675.

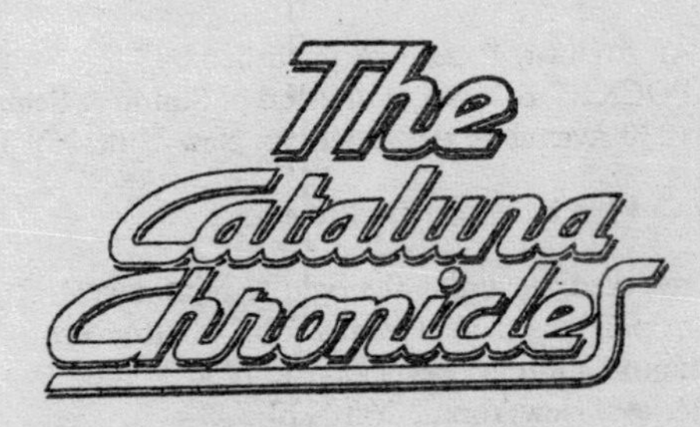


# The Dark Secret

A Parachute Press Book

AN ARCHWAY PAPERBACK
Published by POCKET BOOKS
New York London Toronto Sydney Tokyo Singapore

The sale of this book without its cover is unauthorized. If you purchased this book without a cover, you should be aware that it was reported to the publisher as "unsold and destroyed." Neither the author nor the publisher has received payment for the sale of this "stripped book."

This book is a work of fiction. Names, characters, places and incidents are products of the author's imagination or are used fictitiously. Any resemblance to actual events or locales or persons, living or dead, is entirely coincidental.

AN ARCHWAY PAPERBACK *Original*

An Archway Paperback published by
POCKET BOOKS, a division of Simon & Schuster Inc.
1230 Avenue of the Americas, New York, NY 10020

Copyright © 1995 by Parachute Press, Inc.

All rights reserved, including the right to reproduce this book or portions thereof in any form whatsoever.
For information address Pocket Books, 1230 Avenue of the Americas, New York, NY 10020

ISBN: 0-671-89434-X

First Archway Paperback printing September 1995

10 9 8 7 6 5 4 3 2 1

FEAR STREET is a registered trademark of Parachute Press, Inc.

AN ARCHWAY PAPERBACK and colophon are registered trademarks of Simon & Schuster Inc.

Cover art by Don Brautigam

Printed in the U.S.A.

IL 7+

# prologue

*Cataluna . . .*

My own car, Kurt Masters thought. Yes!

Long and sleek. Gleaming white. All graceful curves and raw power.

Kurt still couldn't believe his parents had given him a car for his seventeenth birthday. He'd been expecting the usual. Some CDs. Some clothes. Maybe a laptop computer to bring with him to college next year.

He ran his hand along the front fender. Kurt could almost hear the deep thrum of the engine as the car responded to his every command.

Soon, he told himself. Soon I'll be behind that wheel.

But first he needed to fix the oil leak.

His dad and mom had surprised him with the white sports car that morning. They noticed the leak then.

No problem, he told his father. Probably the oil plug needs tightening.

Kurt knew cars. He turned toward the toolbox. A smudge on the Cataluna's fender caught his eye.

Funny. I didn't notice that before, he muttered.

He licked his finger and ran it across the small red mark. As he rubbed, the mark grew brighter and more distinct. Not a smudge. A perfect crescent moon.

"Cataluna," he whispered. "Luna . . . moon. Yes, that's it." The car displayed its signature right there on the fender.

Kurt reached for the socket wrench, then changed his mind.

A crescent wrench, he told himself, grinning. That's the kind to use on a car with a crescent moon.

Kurt lay down on the wooden mechanic's cradle and rolled himself under the chassis. He found the oil pan and hung a lamp beside it.

That's strange, he thought. The plug at the bottom of the pan appeared perfectly clean. The entire chassis spotless.

He moved back and forth, searching for the leak. Not a grease mark anywhere, even though his father had bought the car used.

"It must be the oil plug."

He rolled back into position and reached for it.

"Ow!" He jerked his finger away.

Why is it hot? he asked himself. The car hadn't been

driven since the night before. His father had sneaked it into the garage so that Kurt wouldn't see it until the next day. His seventeenth birthday.

Kurt tightened the crescent wrench around the plug.

Someone laughed. Low and teasing. A girl.

"Mom?" he called. No, she's at work, he reminded himself.

He glanced at the garage door.

Closed.

The laughter grew louder. From inside the car. From right above him.

Could the radio be on? he wondered. Maybe something's wrong with the electrical system?

He'd check it out as soon as he tightened this plug.

The wrench slipped off. He started to reposition it, then jerked back his hand. "No way!"

He could have sworn the plug had turned. On its own.

The strange laughter sounded closer.

The car began to rock.

Kurt shoved the cradle back. The wheels jammed.

The car rocked harder. The tires lifting off the ground and slamming back down.

Kurt flung himself off the cradle.

Above him the plug began to turn.

The laughter grew louder. Cruel laughter. Frightening.

Kurt struggled to get out from under the rocking car.

The plug turned again. Kurt let out a shriek.

A boiling stream of oil shot down into his left eye. The black liquid bubbled in his eye socket.

His body jerked and twitched as the scorching liquid sprayed over his face.

Into his nose.

Into his mouth. Scalding him, his tongue, his whole mouth, until it felt as if his head were on fire.

Burning. Burning. The flesh melting from his skull.

Kurt's legs twitched a final time.

And then lay still.

The car stood motionless in the middle of the garage. The only movement the steaming, bubbling oil spreading around Kurt's body.

A river of blood flowed out from under the car. It ran alongside the oil, forming a red crescent moon.

On his seventeenth birthday Kurt Masters became one of the many victims of the evil Cataluna.

But not the first.

That honor belongs to me—William Parker.

I first set eyes upon the strange white car not on the streets of Shadyside. Nor even in the twentieth century.

No, I first gazed upon the Cataluna three centuries before. In the small New England colony of West Hampshire.

The colony had fallen on hard times. The crops withered in the fields, and animals lay dying everywhere.

We in the colony knew only one way to bring our

bad luck to an end. Destroy the cause. Catherine Hatchett. A girl born under a bad moon.

But no ordinary girl. Her mother had been born under the same bad moon. She taught her daughter the dark and secret arts.

When we came for Catherine and dragged her to the hanging tree, she transformed herself into a rat small enough to escape the noose. Then she transformed into a sleek white horse and raced away.

But only after murdering my brother and my father.

I swore I would hunt her down and have my revenge.

# *part*

# 1

## *West Hampshire Colony*
## 1698

# chapter 1

A cold autumn wind swept across the burned-out field, rattling the charred stalks of corn. The odor of smoke hung in the air. The odor of death. The only sign of life—the distant hoot of an owl.

William Parker pulled back the hood of his cloak and grasped a handful of ash. Crushing it in his fist, he watched as it sifted through his fingers and blew away on the wind.

"Catherine . . ." he muttered, raising his eyes toward the sliver of moon in the early evening sky. "This is your handiwork—your *art.*"

"First my brother, Joseph, and then my father. How many others have you killed by now? How many more must die?"

William noticed a dark form at the edge of the field.

His skin turned cold. Fighting back the fear, he cautiously approached.

The smell of death grew stronger.

Yes, Catherine is near, he thought. Very near.

William heard a low cry. He reached for the long-bladed knife at his belt and rushed forward.

A cow lay on its side, moaning in pain. Claw marks slashed its neck and sides. Its belly had been torn open. Glistening pink intestines spilled from the jagged wound.

A shudder ripped through the creature, then it lay still.

An animal did this, but no ordinary one, William knew. Ordinary animals killed for food. There had been no purpose to this killing. Except death itself.

"I shall find you, Catherine of the Moon, Cataluna," William declared, turning from the ugly scene.

Catherine cannot have traveled far since she attacked the poor creature, William thought.

Perhaps he could find settlers nearby. Perhaps they would know of the girl—the creature—he hunted. Even if they did not, it would be good to talk to other people. He had been alone too long.

William gazed across the fields. Where would I build a farmhouse on this land? he asked himself. There at the base of the mountains, he decided. The house would be sheltered from the wind and bathed by sunlight.

"Exactly right," William whispered when he spotted a ramshackle barn.

As he drew closer, a house came into view. Shabby. But some clothes hung on a line and an ax protruded from an upright log. A wagon stood out front.

William felt a surge of excitement at discovering these signs of life. Normal, everyday life. He had been traveling for so long. Across so many miles of wilderness. And now he had found people living in the shadow of the mountains.

He imagined sitting before a warm fireplace. Sharing a cup of tea. Being greeted by a friendly face.

He imagined forgetting about his quest. If even for a few days. A few hours.

William hurried to the front door. He knocked. No answer.

He unlatched the door. It swung open. "Hello," he called in.

William waited for his eyes to grow accustomed to the dim room. He could make out shapes on the floor. Furniture, no doubt. He wondered if there might be a lamp on one of the tables.

Something cold wrapped itself around William's ankle. Cold and smooth.

William tried to jerk his foot away. He fell facedown on the hard floor. He lifted his head—and uttered a shrill scream.

Two blank eyes stared at him. No. Not eyes. Eye sockets.

A skull lay before him. A human skull. Strips of skin still clinging to it. Small white maggots feasting on the putrid flesh.

William stared around frantically. The shapes on the floor were not furniture. Not furniture. They were corpses. All corpses. The flesh rotting away from the bones.

The cold, smooth thing on William's ankle moved. Began to slither up his leg.

# chapter 2

William stared down at his leg. "Noooo!" he shrieked.

A huge black snake coiled around his thigh. Enormous head swaying from side to side. Long, razor-sharp fangs gleaming.

William kicked his leg violently. The snake's coils squeezed harder. Tighter. Its powerful jaws lay too close to William's knife. He needed another weapon.

William groped the floor. Frantically searching for something he could use to defend himself. Anything.

The snake hissed. Prepared to strike.

William's fingers brushed something slick and hard. A human leg bone. Chunks of rotting flesh hanging from it.

Gritting his teeth, William yanked the leg bone

from the corpse. He raised it high over his head. Smashed it down on the black serpent with all his might.

The creature reared back, loosening its grip. Its forked tongue darted between sharp fangs. Fangs glistening with venom. Its dark, beady eyes fixed on William with an evil glare.

William jabbed at the snake with the bone. The creature caught the bone between its jaws. Snapped it like a twig.

The snake lunged at William's throat. William grabbed it below the head. He shoved his thumbs deep into the cold flesh.

The writhing snake uncoiled itself from his leg. It pushed itself down on him. Its fangs inches from his throat.

William squeezed harder. His fingers cramped.

"Die!" he grunted. "Die!"

The creature hissed. Its tail whipped back and forth. It jerked once, twice. And then it hung limp from William's hands.

Again and again William shook the creature. It did not move. He hurled it to the floor.

Breathing hard, William reached for his knife. He wanted to cut off the serpent's head.

William's hand trembled as he pulled the knife from its sheath.

A strangled hiss sliced through the room. The snake clamped its jaws around his hand. Buried its fangs deep in William's skin.

Cold swept up William's arm. His fingers grew numb.

The knife clattered from his grasp. He felt the venom spreading through him as he fell onto his side.

The serpent slinked away. It slithered through the rib cage of the skeleton and curled up on the floor.

William's vision blurred. Grew cloudy. He struggled to keep the snake in sight.

The serpent coiled into a ball. Legs and razor claws popped out from its belly. Hard scales melted into sleek black fur.

Before William's eyes, the snake became a cat.

The cat arched its back and purred. Its purr became a throaty growl. It stared at William with cold eyes.

The eyes of Catherine of the Moon.

The cat hunched low. Motionless. Eyeing its prey. Its fangs dripped blood. William's blood.

William tried to move. Too numb. Too slow.

He heard a hiss.

The creature sprang through the air. Claws out, aimed at his eyes.

# chapter 3

William forced his hands up to cover his face. He waited for the pain of claws slashing across his flesh.

He remembered Catherine Hatchett taking the form of a cat and blinding his brother, Joseph. Digging out Joseph's eyeballs with her claws.

William heard a thump. The creature had leaped over him.

The cat's growl became a piercing laugh. The laughter of a girl.

"I have won, William Parker! I have won!"

William rolled over to face her. He blinked his eyes. The blurred image took the shadowy form of a girl. A girl he recognized.

"You have tasted my venom," Catherine Hatchett declared. She folded her arms across her chest. "Now you shall die!"

William tried to speak. His throat felt dry and tight. Each breath a struggle. His lungs burning from the snake poison.

"You and your friends used to laugh at me. You called me Bad Moon Catherine. But now who is the one born under a bad moon?"

"I . . . I—" he stammered, trying to keep his head from dropping to the floor.

"Save your words for someone who cares!" she exclaimed, moving toward him, her body beginning to transform. "Save them for your father and brother. Maybe they will listen. When you join them in death!"

William could barely keep his eyes open. Catherine's cat fur brushed his cheek. A throaty purr close beside his ear.

He tried to speak, but no words would come.

"Goodbye, William. Sleep forever."

The cat faded silently into the night.

The room turned colder. Blacker. William felt the venom pulsing through him, spreading through his body. He fought the urge to sleep.

*I will not die!* he vowed to himself.

*You will not escape me so easily, Cataluna. I will not—I cannot—die! I swear that I will hunt you down! And the evil you have brought to others will be the evil that destroys you!*

His mind swirled. His thoughts foggy and unclear.

His body grew lighter. Seemed to lift off the floor. He tried to grab something, anything. But his hands would not respond.

William was floating now. Flying. Fading into the night.

He forced open his eyelids. *No!* he raged. *It is only magic! Catherine's magic! I will not be killed by magic!*

William concentrated on taking small, steady breaths.

*Yes, I will survive! I will overcome her dark magic and survive!*

"I . . . I w-will not d-die!" he sputtered, his lips able to move again.

He pushed himself onto his knees. Shook his head to clear it.

His chest heaved. His breath painful. The air burning his lungs.

William stared up at the ceiling. Noticed a spider weaving its web. He gazed at the spider and thought of Catherine, the Cat of the Moon.

"You will not escape me so easily," he whispered.

William forced himself to his feet. His legs trembled, but he did not fall.

"I will hunt you down!" William vowed. "Your evil will not go unpunished."

William's voice grew louder. Stronger. He raised his fist into the air.

"I will destroy you, Cataluna!"

# *part* 2

## *Shadyside* 1995

# chapter 4

Justin Norris crammed two chocolate chip cookies into his mouth. He chewed loudly. Crumbs fell over his flannel shirt.

"Very attractive," Lauren Patterson commented. She glanced over at her stepsister, Regina. "You go out in public with this guy?"

"Yes, but I keep him on a leash, and he's a very good boy. Aren't you, Justin?" Regina patted her boyfriend on the head like a dog. Her bright pink nail polish gleamed against his dark blond hair.

Justin grinned and panted like a dog. He jumped off the couch and crouched down on all fours. "Woof!" He grabbed one of Regina's clogs in his teeth and shook it.

She swatted him on the nose. "Bad dog!"

Justin crawled over to Lauren and rolled onto his back. Arms and legs up in the air. He gave a pathetic little whimper. Stared at Lauren with his dark green eyes.

Regina snorted. "He wants you to scratch his belly, Lauren. The doggie likes you," she told her stepsister.

"Oh, gross," Lauren groaned.

Lauren felt her face grow hot. She never knew quite how to handle Justin's teasing.

"You do it, Regina. You're his girlfriend," Lauren added quickly.

Regina held up her hands. "I'm not ruining my manicure!"

Justin gave Lauren another pitiful glance. He whined like a puppy.

Is Justin flirting with me? Lauren wondered.

No way, she told herself immediately. He's Regina's boyfriend. He wouldn't flirt with me in front of her.

Besides, what guy would flirt with me with Regina around? She's a zillion times prettier.

I'm so ordinary-looking. Ordinary brown hair. Ordinary brown eyes. Ordinary everything.

Regina and Lauren's dog, Spot, trotted over and licked Justin's face. Justin rolled over and climbed back on all fours.

"There's a new dog on the block," he called to Spot. "You're dead meat. I'm Hulk Hound Dog, champion dog wrestler."

Spot wagged his tail. Regina and Lauren glanced at each other and started to giggle.

"You want a piece of me, Spot. Well, come and get it. It's suppertime." Justin grabbed Spot and playfully pinned him to the floor. "He's down for the count. It doesn't look good, folks."

Justin grabbed Spot's back legs. He pulled out a rubber band from his pocket and tied the dog's back paws together.

Spot yelped in protest.

"But wait!" Justin cried. "He's up again."

Spot dragged himself across the floor. His back legs useless. The dog began to whimper.

"He's hurt, but he's not going to let Hulk—"

"Stop it!" Regina yelled. "Justin, you always go too far."

Lauren ran over to the dog. She gently pulled the rubber band off Spot's legs.

"Very cool, Justin," Lauren said sarcastically. "I'm so impressed. You can win a fight with a twenty-pound dog." She tenderly rubbed Spot's head.

"Hey," Justin muttered. "We were playing. He's not hurt."

"No thanks to you," Lauren snapped. "Come on, Spot." She strode out of the living room and into the kitchen.

Lauren grabbed a Coke from the refrigerator. What does Regina see in that guy? she asked herself. Okay, he's cute. In a grungy, Christian Slater kind of way. But he has a sick sense of humor. And he's gotten kicked out of school more than once. She popped the top off the Coke can and gulped down a long swallow.

Regina could have her pick of guys, Lauren thought. With her long, curly red hair. Great bod. And the clothes to show it off.

Lauren's stepsister was gorgeous—and knew it.

Lauren had to fight Regina for bathroom time every morning. Regina spent hours on her hair and makeup. She had photos of models taped all over the mirror to give her ideas.

Regina constantly nagged Lauren to spend more time on her makeup and clothes. She offered to loan Lauren any of her Betsey Johnson mini-dresses.

But Lauren preferred her own jeans and sneakers.

Almost time for Mom to arrive home, Lauren realized. She tugged at her brown bangs. A nervous habit.

Regina better get Justin out of here. Justin made the top ten list of things that drove their mother crazy.

Lauren wandered back into the living room. She found Justin and Regina in a major lip lock. Justin's hands caught in Regina's red hair.

"Umm-hum." Lauren stared at the floor. She always felt embarrassed when she walked in on Justin and Regina kissing.

Her sister didn't bother to open her eyes. "What," she mumbled against Justin's lips.

"You have about fifteen minutes to Mom—and counting," Lauren replied. Regina and Justin broke their kiss. Justin had Regina's Strawberry Sensation lipstick smeared on his mouth.

"Better get going, Justin," Lauren advised.

A car door slammed.

"She's early!" Regina cried. She grabbed Justin's arm and started hauling him to the back door. "Out. Out. Out."

"Wait. My backpack!" Justin protested.

The key turned in the lock of the front door.

Lauren lunged for the backpack.

The front door swung open.

The back door closed with a click.

"Lauren, I'm so glad you're home." Mrs. Patterson stood in the doorway smiling at her. "Where's Regina?"

Lauren eased the backpack behind her. She started to reply when the kitchen door opened and Regina sauntered in.

"Hi, Mom," she called casually. She plopped down on the sofa. Straightened one of her thigh-high socks.

"What's that?" Mrs. Patterson asked. She motioned at the backpack, not quite hidden behind Lauren's back.

Regina stared at Lauren pleadingly.

"Oh, this?" Lauren lifted it in front of her and clutched it in her arms. "It's Sue's. She stopped by after school and forgot it." She heard Regina's sigh of relief. "I'll take it to her house later."

"Why not drive it over there now?"

Lauren glanced at her stepsister. "I, uh . . . I've got homework to do."

"Forget your homework. Go out for a drive. Both of you."

Mom telling her to forget homework? Lauren couldn't believe it.

"Sounds fun," Regina replied. "Are you coming, Lauren?" she asked from the open front door.

"Uh, sure." Lauren slung the backpack over her shoulder.

"Aren't you girls forgetting something?" Mrs. Patterson asked. "The car keys?"

"I've got mine." Regina jingled her key ring.

"Not *this* one."

Mrs. Patterson held out a key. Lauren stared at it. Then she stared at Regina. "You *didn't!*" Lauren gasped.

"Your father and I always said that when you both turned sixteen—"

*"Yes!"* Regina cried. She rushed forward and snatched the key.

Lauren gazed at the key as Regina turned it over and over in her hand. Shining mother-of-pearl circled the top. "We never believed you were serious."

"Neither did I," Mrs. Patterson replied with a laugh. "But I thought you'd be more interested in the car than the key."

"It's here?" Lauren yelped.

"In the driveway."

Regina dashed through the doorway. Lauren close on her heels. They couldn't see the driveway until they circled the hedge alongside the garage.

"It . . . it's . . ." Regina began.

"Unbelievable!" Lauren blurted out. She pushed past Regina and cautiously approached.

Long and low and sleek. As white as the moon. The most incredible sports car Lauren had ever seen. Had ever imagined.

"I know what you're thinking," Mrs. Patterson told them, placing an arm around each of her daughters. "Robert and I said you couldn't have a sports car. But when we found it, I guess we both lost our heads."

"It's perfect!" Lauren declared, beaming at her mother.

"It's a Cataluna," Mrs. Patterson told them.

"I've never heard of it," Regina replied.

Mrs. Patterson pointed to a small red mark on the right front fender. In the shape of a crescent moon. "The Cataluna's signature," she explained.

"I love it!" Regina cried.

"Me, too," Lauren breathed.

"Are you sure? You don't mind that we picked it without you?"

In reply, the girls threw their arms around her and kissed her cheeks.

They raced over to the car. Regina still held the key, so she grabbed the driver's seat.

Lauren jumped into the passenger side and rolled down her window. Mrs. Patterson leaned in. "Keep away from the downtown traffic until you get a feel for how she handles. And be careful shifting gears. And wear your seat belts."

"Go on," Lauren prodded her sister.

Regina turned the key. The engine responded instantly, settling into a low, steady hum.

"Here we go!" Regina exclaimed.

She backed slowly down the driveway. Eased out onto Fear Street.

Lauren leaned against the red leather seat. She barely heard her mother's final words of caution. She listened to the throaty purr of the engine. Smelled the supple leather. Felt the wind against her face.

Regina turned left onto Mill Road. Left again onto Hawthorne Drive.

Lauren closed her eyes. She imagined them cruising down a road to nowhere. To somewhere. To anywhere but Shadyside.

The wind whipped Lauren's hair. The engine roared as Regina shifted gears.

Lauren opened her eyes. Too fast, she thought.

Way too fast.

She glanced over at the speedometer. Forty-five. Fifty. Fifty-five.

"Regina, better slow down," Lauren said.

They sped down a residential street. Cars parked along the curb. Kids and bikes in the yards.

"Regina!" she repeated. "Slow down!" Her stepsister didn't seem to hear.

Regina stared straight ahead. Her fingers white as she clenched the wheel.

"What's your problem? Slow down!" Lauren cried. "Slow down! Don't you hear me?"

Something moved in the corner of Lauren's vision. She gaped into the windshield.

Up ahead, a girl on Rollerblades skated into the street.

Into the path of the Cataluna.

"Regina! Stop!" Lauren shrieked.

# chapter

# 5

The brakes squealed. The horn blared.

They skidded out of control, first to the left, then the right.

Lauren glimpsed arms and legs flailing. Flying through the air. She threw her hands over her eyes.

Finally the car screeched to a halt.

Lauren jerked off her seat belt. Pushed open the door and staggered out of the car on shaky legs.

*Please,* let her be all right! she prayed as she searched for the girl. Let her still be alive!

Lauren heard someone laughing.

Teasing, throaty laughter. A girl.

Lauren spun around and gaped at her stepsister. Regina leaned against the car trunk. Laughing. "Did you see her jump?" Regina cried.

The young skater stood on a lawn nearby. Brushing herself off.

"You're all right!" Lauren exclaimed. She rushed over and knelt in front of the girl, who appeared to be about eight. "Are you hurt?"

"I . . . I don't think so."

"Were you hit?"

The girl shook her head, then muttered, "I-I'm sorry."

Lauren threw her arms around the girl. "It wasn't your fault. We didn't see you."

Regina approached, and Lauren shot her an angry glance.

"Please don't tell my mother," the girl pleaded. She sniffled but forced back her tears. "She's always saying to stay out of the street. If she finds out . . ."

"Don't worry. We won't tell anyone," Lauren reassured her.

"Of course not, kid." Regina cuffed her playfully on the chin. "You did a great flip on those skates."

"I did?" She gave a half smile.

"Like a pro." Regina turned to Lauren. "Let's get going."

I can't believe she's walking away, Lauren thought. She turned back to the girl. "What's your name?"

"Samantha . . . Sammy."

"Are you sure you're all right, Sammy?"

The little girl smiled and nodded.

"You'd better go home, then."

She gave Samantha a gentle nudge and watched as she skated gingerly down the sidewalk.

"Come on!" Regina called from behind the wheel.

"You're lucky," Lauren declared, climbing into the car.

"Skill, not luck," Regina insisted. "It's all in the wrists." Giggling, she started the engine.

Lauren gaped at her in amazement. "How can you laugh? You almost hit that little girl."

Regina waved off the remark. "Don't be such a wimp. She wasn't hurt." Regina stepped on the gas and pulled out into the street.

"You could have killed her. Or somebody else."

"But I didn't." She gave Lauren a sly smile. Regina revved the engine. Taunting her sister.

"Regina! Don't!"

"Don't worry, I'll drive just like Grandma." Regina hunched over the wheel and squinted. The car slowed to a crawl.

"You're terrible!" Lauren muttered, trying not to grin.

"Hang on!" Regina gave the Cataluna some gas. As the sports car lurched forward, she threw back her head and laughed. "This car is fun!"

"Five messages on my answering machine. You left five!"

"Marcy, you're back!" Lauren exclaimed. She flopped down on her bed and held the receiver against her ear.

"That's right, genius," her best friend teased. "And I demand to know what happened worthy of five messages. Oh, I know. Regina's boyfriend got suspended again? No. That's about a three-messager. Ryan asked you out? No. That's probably a six. You—"

"I got a car!" Lauren interrupted. "Well, Regina and I got a car," she added. "And I had to wait two whole days to tell you."

"Details! I need details!" Marcy urged.

"It's a Cataluna."

"Never heard of it," Marcy replied.

"Me, either. Its a sports car. White with a little red crescent moon on the front fender. Bloodred leather seats," Lauren told her.

"I told you your horoscope promised a surprise this week. I have to see it. I'll be right over," Marcy announced.

"No. I'll pick you up. We'll go for a ride," Lauren answered.

"Great." Marcy hung up without saying goodbye.

Lauren hung up the phone and grabbed her sweater. She hurried down to the kitchen and snatched her keys off the table.

"Where are you off to?" Mrs. Patterson asked, glancing up from the salad she was making.

"To show Marcy the new car. She just got back," Lauren explained.

"Dinner's at seven."

"I'll be home by then," Lauren promised. She opened the door.

"Oh, Lauren. While you're out, would you pick up some milk? There's none for breakfast."

"It's Regina's turn to run errands," Lauren reminded her.

"I know. But she's grounded. Robert caught her driving around with Justin when she told us she'd be studying at Darlene's."

Regina had been spending even more time with Justin than usual. Racing around in the Cataluna.

"Justin-itis," Lauren muttered. Regina's got a fatal disease.

"What?" her mother asked.

"How much milk do you want?"

"A half-gallon," Mrs. Patterson replied. "Skim, okay?"

"You got it," Lauren called on her way out the door.

Lauren hurried to the driveway. She couldn't wait to show Marcy the car. She rounded the hedge.

And stopped.

"No," she whispered.

"No! Someone's stolen the Cataluna!"

# chapter 6

Lauren dived to the garage and hoisted up the door.

No Cataluna.

"Mom!" she screamed, running back into the house. "The car! It's been stolen!"

Mrs. Patterson glanced up from the kitchen counter. "Huh? Stolen? What are you talking about, Lauren?"

"The Cataluna! It's gone! It's not in the driveway—or the garage."

Wiping her hands on a dish towel, Mrs. Patterson hurried out of the kitchen. Down the hallway to Regina's room. She rapped on the door. "Regina, are you in there?"

*Oh, no!* Lauren thought as she followed her mother. *Regina's going to kill me. She must have sneaked out.*

"Regina," Mrs. Patterson called again. No response. She pushed the door open. The room was empty.

Mrs. Patterson crossed the room and shut the half-open window. "I swear, Robert and I will have to put bars on this room!"

"Don't be mad," Lauren begged, coming up beside her mother. "I'm sure she had a good reason."

"A reason named Justin," her mother muttered angrily.

"Come on, Mom. You don't know she's with Justin," Lauren said.

"I don't?" Mrs. Patterson pointed out the window.

Lauren peered out onto the road. The Cataluna stood parked halfway down Fear Street. Justin climbed out. He leaned back through the window and gave Regina a long kiss. Then he waved and ran off.

The car started forward and turned into their driveway.

Lauren felt sick to her stomach. *If I'd kept my mouth shut, Regina wouldn't be in trouble,* she told herself. *I'm such an idiot. How could I have thought someone stole the car?*

Mrs. Patterson opened the window again, then backed across the bedroom. Waited with her arms folded across her chest.

Lauren retreated to the doorway. Watched in silence as her stepsister appeared at the window.

Regina pulled herself over the windowsill. Into the room. And found her mother standing there.

"M-Mom!" she stammered. She scrambled the rest of the way into the room. "I needed a notebook from Darlene—"

"Don't make it worse, Regina," her mother ordered. "I *saw* you out there with him."

She motioned to Lauren. "We both did."

"But you don't understand," Regina protested.

"I understand perfectly. Now here's something for you to understand. I do not want you to have any contact with Justin Norris."

"But, Mom, it's not Justin's fault I sneaked out," Regina pleaded.

"You never acted this way before you started going out with him," her mother replied. "I don't want him coming over here. I don't want you driving around with him. I don't want you talking to him on the phone."

"That's so unfair!" Regina wailed.

"Was it fair to climb out the window when you were grounded? Was it fair to lie to me?" Mrs. Patterson didn't wait for an answer. She turned and strode out of the room.

Lauren stepped inside and quietly closed the door behind her. "She'll get over it, Reg. You'll probably be able to go out with Justin in a few weeks. You know how she is when she's mad."

Regina's eyes narrowed. "Don't pretend to be sorry it happened. You filthy little snitch." Her lips quivered with rage.

"Excuse me?" Lauren cried.

"Mom said you were staring out the window at me," Regina shouted. "What's the matter, Lauren? Unhappy because you don't have a boyfriend of your own?"

"Shut up, Regina. Shut up."

"No. That's it, right? You don't have a boyfriend of your own. So you spend all your time spying on me with mine. Have any nice fantasies, Lauren? Fantasies of Justin kissing you instead of me?"

"You know that's not true!" Lauren protested.

"Get *out* of here!" Regina yelled. "I can't stand the sound of your voice. I can't stand anything about you."

Regina pulled open the bedroom door. "Leave!"

She shoved Lauren out. Slammed the door in her face.

Lauren unhappily trudged to her own room. She shut the door and dropped down on the bed.

What's wrong with Regina? she asked herself. She should know I wouldn't try to get her in trouble. I covered for her when Justin left his backpack in the living room.

I've covered for her lots of times.

Lauren flopped back on the bed. I didn't do anything wrong! Why do I feel so horrible?

She rolled over onto her side. A picture of the two of them stood on the nightstand. Both eight years old. Both in their little bridesmaid dresses for their parents' wedding.

Lauren felt so happy that day. She had hated being

an only child. She remembered dreaming about having a sister. She thought it would be like going to a slumber party every night.

And sometimes it was. She and Regina talked about all kinds of stuff. Guys. Parents. School. Everything.

Sure, they had had fights before. But Regina had never been so cruel. So vicious.

*What is wrong?* Lauren wondered. *Why is Regina acting so strange?*

"Regina, slow down," Lauren pleaded.

"Give me a break. I'm not going that fast."

Lauren glanced at the speedometer.

Only forty-five.

"What should I do?" Regina muttered, under her breath. "What should I do?"

"About what?" Lauren asked.

"About Justin," Regina snapped. "He's always pressuring me to sneak over to his house."

Lauren checked the speedometer again.

Fifty.

"If I don't find a way to go out with Justin, he'll start dating other girls. I know it. Justin's not the type to stay home by himself."

Regina pushed down on the gas pedal.

"This whole thing is your fault, Lauren. Why did you snitch on me?"

"Regina, I explained it to you. I know it sounds stupid. But I really thought someone stole the car."

Her sister snorted and rolled her eyes. "Yeah, right."

Lauren sighed. "I should have checked your room before I said anything to Mom. I should have. But I panicked. Come on. I already apologized. What do you want from me?"

Regina ignored her and pushed down on the gas pedal.

"I want you to stay out of my life."

"Fine," Lauren replied coldly. "But you have to slow down or we're not going to have a life."

Regina pushed down on the gas pedal.

"What's wrong with you?" Lauren shouted. "You never used to drive like this!"

Regina laughed. "It's fun! Something you don't know anything about, Lauren."

A tricycle rolled into the street.

Lauren frantically grabbed the dashboard.

A little boy in bright red overalls ran after the trike.

*"Stop!"* Lauren shrieked. She tried to grab the wheel.

Regina laughed. She spun the wheel hard to the right.

Aimed straight toward the trike.

"Stop!" Lauren screamed out the car window at the boy. "Stop! Stop! Stop!"

But the boy came running after his tricycle.

Lauren shut her eyes—as a sickening crack shook the car.

# chapter 7

Regina slammed on the brakes.

Lauren spun around. The little boy knelt beside his mangled tricycle. Crying. But unhurt.

Regina laughed, her eyes flashing with excitement.

"You're *crazy!*" Lauren shrieked. "You deliberately—"

"What are you talking about?" Regina grinned at Lauren. "That trike rolled right out in front of us."

"Yes, but—"

"We'd better get out of here," Regina warned. "I think the kid's mother is on her way."

Regina jammed the gear stick into first and stepped on the gas. The car roared away, tires spinning, kicking up a cloud of smoke.

"What's *wrong* with you, Regina?" Lauren demanded.

"The kid's okay. He'll know better than to push his trike out into the street next time." Regina snickered to herself.

Lauren turned to the passenger window. She couldn't believe what she'd heard. "It isn't funny. You could've run over that boy. Last week you almost hit that skater. And all you can do is laugh? How can you think it's funny?"

"It's not me laughing," Regina claimed. "It's the car."

"Excuse me? The *car?"*

"Yes. The radio. Don't you hear that girl on the radio? She's the one laughing."

Lauren glanced at the radio.

Off.

Something's very wrong with Regina, Lauren thought. Is she cracking up, having some kind of breakdown?

"Pull over, Regina," she ordered, shaking her head to clear it. "Let me drive."

Regina didn't even glance at her.

Lauren leaned over and grabbed her arm.

"Get off!" Regina snapped, slapping away Lauren's hand.

"Stop!" Lauren demanded.

"Leave me alone! I'm driving this car!" Regina screamed.

"Okay. Okay," Lauren said soothingly. It's probably more dangerous to try and make her stop, she thought.

Regina threw back her head and laughed.

So cold-hearted. So cruel.

Lauren shivered.

I'm afraid of her, Lauren realized. I'm afraid of Regina. I'm afraid of my own sister.

Lauren drove slowly past the North Hills Country Club. The wind swept back her brown bangs.

She felt the tension of the past several days fly away.

She and her sister had barely spoken to each other for a week, since the day Regina ran into the trike.

That horrible day. The day Lauren realized she felt afraid of Regina.

Lauren found herself watching Regina all the time now. Studying her.

Questions constantly ran through Lauren's mind. Is Regina sick? Should I talk to Mom and Dad about her? Or will that only make things worse?

One question returned again and again. Is Regina dangerous?

*"Let's go faster, Lauren!"* a voice cried.

Now I'm hearing things. Lauren shook her head and concentrated on the road.

*"Come on! Let's have some fun!"* A girl's voice. Soft, but excited.

"Regina—is that you?" Lauren asked. "Is this some kind of trick?"

She glanced at the passenger seat. Empty.

She peered over her shoulder into the backseat. Empty.

*"Let's move!"* the voice urged.

Lauren twisted the knob on the radio. Off.

*"It's easy! Just push your foot down on the pedal!"*

"Who's there?" Lauren cried. "What do you want?"

*"Step on the gas, Lauren! Let's have some fun!"*

# *part*

# 3

## *West Hampshire Colony*

## 1698

## *chapter* 8

William forced himself not to think about the hunger gnawing at his belly. He did not know when he would find food again. Or how he would catch it with only the knife tucked in his belt.

He had slowly recovered from the venom of the snakebite. From Catherine Hatchett's dark magic.

It had taken several days, days of fever and chills. Days of frightening dreams. Finally the fever had departed, leaving him weak but eager to continue his quest.

For three days he had been pursuing Catherine west. Following the paw prints of a cat.

He had eaten nothing but a few pieces of dried beef. Drunk nothing but drops of dew captured on leaves.

And then the trail ran out. So did his food.

Would my father and brother want me to spend my life tracking this creature? he asked himself. If I find her and kill her, they will still be dead.

But William knew that he would never find peace until he destroyed Catherine of the Moon. Cataluna. How could he make a life for himself knowing her evil continued killing to live?

William lost track of the days. Occasionally he came upon a stream where he eased his thirst. His only food—nuts and roots.

Days became weeks. Leaves withered and fell from the trees. The frigid wind blasted down on him. Heavy clouds threatened snow.

William grew weaker. Not Catherine's magic this time, he told himself. Death.

Death stalked him, and he knew it would catch him. He would die if he did not find shelter before the first snows arrived.

The storm struck without warning. It began with lightning and rain. Sheets of hail that gashed his face and hands. Then silent, blinding snow. Drifting piles of deadly white.

William staggered onward. When he could walk no more, he dropped to his knees. Crawled through the drifts on all fours.

He rolled onto his back and stared up at the hazy, snow-swept sky.

Sleep, he thought. I must sleep.

Sleep will bring relief.

His vision grew dark as a shadow passed over him. The shadow of a cloaked figure. Death? he wondered.

The figure pulled back the hood of the cloak. William gazed upon an angelic face. If this is death, let it take me, he thought.

"Are you all right?" a voice called through the whipping wind. Not the voice of death. The voice of a girl.

Gentle hands lifted his head from the snow. Rubbed his cheeks to bring back the warmth. The life.

"You must get up!" she urged, tugging at him.

"Wh-who are you?" he stammered, trying to focus on her.

"Evie. My name is Evie. Don't try to talk. Save your strength. We must bring you out of this storm."

He struggled to his feet. Felt her arm wrap around him as she helped him through the drifts.

The flickering lights of a farmhouse grew closer. At last the door opened and he stumbled inside.

The blast of heat made his head spin. His legs grew rubbery. He sprawled forward onto the floor.

"Evie . . ." he whispered as the world went black.

William awakened to a beautiful vision. What a wonderful dream, he thought.

A girl gazed down at him with large blue eyes. Her skin soft and clear, her hair the color of spun gold. "Are you feeling better today?"

The girl touched a moist cloth to his forehead, patting it tenderly.

"Wh-where am I?" he stammered, trying to lift his head.

"Rest easy, William," she said soothingly, urging him back against the pillow.

"My name . . . you know my name?"

She smiled. "You spoke it many times in your sleep. And that of your brother, Joseph."

His memories rushed back to him. The murder of his father and brother. The search for Catherine Hatchett. The mysterious girl who saved him in the storm.

"Evie," he whispered. "Joseph is dead. My father is dead."

A tear fell from the corner of her eye. It hit him on the cheek. Warm.

"Where are we?" he asked the girl, who appeared to be a year or two younger than he.

"My father's farm. Near Woodsbridge. My father's name is Henry Mason."

"How long?" William swallowed hard. "How long have I been here?"

"Two days. You had a fever, but it is almost gone."

"I . . ."

"Try not to speak. You must rest and have something to eat. I will bring you some hot soup from the fireplace." She turned to leave, then paused. "Would you bring it for me, Jessica?" she asked.

William gazed beyond the fair-haired girl to the one named Jessica. A little older—seventeen or eighteen, perhaps. Equally beautiful, with olive skin and dark brown eyes. A few stray locks of black hair spilled from beneath the white cap she wore low on her forehead. The cap was securely held in place by ribbons tied in a bow under her chin.

The dark-haired girl nodded. She left the room, pulling the door partway closed.

"That is my cousin, Jessica Mason," Evie explained. "She came to live with us, now that her parents have passed away. I hope she is not sorry."

"Sorry?" he asked.

Evie nodded. "She only recently arrived. She does not talk much. And she always appears so solemn. I think she expected it to be a bit more comfortable here on my father's farm."

She gestured at the room with its bare walls and modest furniture.

"Things used to be better," Evie continued. "But we have had some bad luck these past few weeks. Father recently returned from Woodsbridge. He had to sell many of our possessions."

William felt a stab of fear in his stomach. He remembered the burned-out crops and carcass-littered fields. He remembered Catherine.

The door pushed open. William expected Jessica to enter.

"No," he whispered.

A large black cat padded into the room. It rubbed itself against Evie's long skirts, purring contentedly.

Then it noticed the stranger on the bed. Its purr became a low growl.

William stared as the creature edged closer to the bed. It arched its back slightly. The fur over its spine bristled.

The cat gazed up at him with strange, curious eyes.

Not the eyes of a cat.

The eyes of a girl.

# chapter 9

William Parker and the cat stared at each other, a contest of wills.

Soon William's vision clouded over. He felt dizzy and feared he would faint.

Where am I? he thought.

Back on the floor of that abandoned farmhouse? A rotting skeleton lying beside me? Catherine glowering at me with her evil Cataluna eyes?

Evie Mason's voice cut through the fog in his mind. Sweet, angelic music. "There, there, Raven. Be friendly to our guest."

Bending down, she scooped the cat into her arms. Stroked its long black fur.

"She is a bit of a loner, but she will not harm you."

William blinked to clear his vision. When he

glanced back at the animal, it seemed quite ordinary. With ordinary green cat's eyes and a soft purr.

My imagination is running wild, he thought. These days I find monsters everywhere.

"That is better, Raven," Evie cooed. She placed the animal on the floor and patted its back. "Yes, you are a strange one, Raven. At least we do not have to worry about mice with you around."

William watched the cat rub itself against the leg of the bed. Then it strutted regally across the room.

At the doorway Raven gazed at him a final time. She cocked her head and almost seemed to smile. In her purr he thought he heard a voice.

And then Raven disappeared.

In her place stood Jessica Adams. She cradled a wooden bowl in her hands, steam curling above it.

Lowering her eyes shyly to avoid William's, she handed the bowl to Evie. She whispered something. Too low for William to understand.

"Do not worry. I will let the soup cool a bit," Evie replied. "But please do not wait for me. You and Father start your supper before it gets cold."

"Am I keeping you from supper?" William asked. He eased his legs over the bed and sat up.

"Oh, William, do not get up. You really should be resting."

It has been so long since someone felt concern for me, William thought.

"I feel fine," he assured her. "Really I do. A bit hungry, is all."

A deep voice boomed from the doorway. "So, I find our visitor has awakened!"

William lifted his gaze to a short, powerful man. His hair blond, like his daughter's. He did not smile, yet a touch of merriment twinkled in his eyes.

"Father, this is William," Evie said. She turned back to William. "I am afraid we do not know your last name."

"Parker. William Parker," he replied.

"Pleased to meet you, William," the farmer said jovially. He crossed the room and shook his hand. "I am Henry Mason. I suppose you have been introduced to the girls."

William nodded.

"We are about to sit down to supper. Will you join us?"

Evie laid her hand on her father's forearm. "Perhaps William should be resting?"

"He seems fit enough to me. Are you, William?"

"Yes. I feel fine. And I would enjoy the company. I have spent too many days alone."

Henry clapped him on the shoulder. "A bit hungry, I would bet! One of Evie's suppers will mend that in no time."

Evie's expression betrayed her concern. But then she nodded. "Yes, William. It will do you good."

Jessica stood in the shadows, neither smiling nor frowning. Shyness, no doubt, William told himself.

But the pleasant smiles of the farmer and his daughter were so warm, so inviting. He felt immediately at home. At last he could rest. Forget about his quest. Forget about Catherine. If only for one night.

He gazed up at Evie and grinned. "I would love to have supper with you!" he exclaimed. "I have not had a good meal in . . . in a long time."

"I am afraid all we can offer is simple fare," Evie apologized.

"Our pantry is not what it used to be," Henry admitted. "But Evie can turn a single potato into a meal fit for a king. She will make some man a good wife."

William noticed the way she blushed at the compliment. He turned away so that she would not be embarrassed.

But he could not help thinking about life with a girl like Evie. A life filled with warm smiles and laughter. A life not devoted to revenge.

"I will have to get dressed first." He glanced down at the bedclothes covering him.

"Everything has been washed," Evie assured him. She gestured toward a chair. His clothes sat there in a neat pile.

"Then I will join you in a few minutes."

Henry Mason led his daughter from the room. Jessica followed behind them. William caught her stealing a glance at him. He smiled to put her at ease.

She quickly lowered her gaze and scurried away, closing the door behind her.

That Jessica is a quiet one, he thought.

"Evie." He sighed, enjoying the gentle sound of her name on his lips.

And then his jaw tightened. His eyes narrowed in anger.

No, he told himself. The only girl I should be thinking about right now is Catherine Hatchett.

His hand clenched into a fist.

Catherine, Cat of the Bad Moon.

But the image of Catherine faded into one of Evie. A girl so caring. So beautiful. He had forgotten that such beauty still existed in the world.

He whispered her name again and smiled.

William pushed his plate away. "That is the most delicious meal I have had in a long time," he declared.

Their supper had consisted only of some thin vegetable soup, a small piece of beef, and a slice of bread. But Evie had prepared it with a tasty assortment of spices and herbs.

"Delicious!" Henry Mason exclaimed, patting his belly. "Don't you agree, Jessica?"

The black-haired girl shyly lowered her eyes and nodded. Her face hidden in the shadows of her cap. William thought it strange that she had not removed it during the meal.

She did not speak a word during the entire supper, William realized. No. Longer than that. Not since the moment I met her.

"You should be back in bed, William," Evie insisted. She began to clear the table, and Jessica rose to help.

"I feel fine," he insisted. "Really I do."

"Then perhaps you will join me for a walk," Henry

suggested. He crossed to the door and put on his jacket.

"Yes, I would like to view the farm."

Henry handed him his coat and led the way outside.

The sun had almost set. But William could still make out his surroundings. Not an inviting sight.

A blanket of snow covered the ground. Broken branches littered the yard. The work of the storm, no doubt.

A horse stood tied to a post. He nibbled on a few stray weeds he had managed to uncover. But his ribs stuck out. He appeared not to have eaten in weeks.

"Oh, he has been fed," Henry commented, noticing William staring at the animal. "But he has trouble keeping things down. The flesh will not stay on his bones."

"Getting old, I suppose."

"Only three years old." Henry shook his head sadly. "It is something else. A curse, no doubt."

"Curse?" William asked.

"That is what I call it. We enjoyed fine weather all season. But the crops started dying. Then the cow and chickens. Then Charlie."

"Charlie?"

"The best farmhand I ever hired. He began to sicken. About a week ago he died. Yes, exactly a week. I remember Jessica arrived two days earlier."

He strode toward the field, William at his side.

"Jessica . . . she is your niece?" William asked.

Henry nodded. "My brother Jacob and his wife both died suddenly. Jessica is all they had, so I invited her here." He frowned. "I did not expect her to be full-grown."

"You had not seen her in a long time?"

"I had *never* seen her. Jacob lived in Philadelphia. I have never been south of New York. I knew she would be near seventeen. But somehow I expected a little girl."

"Does she always wear that cap?" William asked.

Henry nodded. "I have been wondering the same thing. She will not take it off. Ever. Claims she feels more comfortable with it on."

Henry stopped and faced the house. "Enough talk of the girls. I brought you out here to ask a question." He clapped his hand on William's shoulder and gave a squeeze.

"Certainly," William replied, feeling slightly uncomfortable. "What is it?"

"Evie is a wonder. Ever since her mother died, she has taken up the load. And done a fine job. But this is a farm, and a farm needs men to work it. I cannot do it by myself."

"It must be hard without Charlie."

"Not just Charlie. Burgess, too. My other worker saw what happened to Charlie. It frightened him. He disappeared the other night. Now I am working the place alone."

He gripped both of William's shoulders and stared him in the eye.

"You do not appear to be the kind of lad who frightens easily. Am I right, William?"

"I would like to think so," he replied, standing a little straighter.

"Then stay and work the farm with me. I cannot pay much. In truth, I cannot pay anything right now. But you will have a roof over your head and some food in your belly."

William hesitated. He had reasons to stay. He felt Catherine's presence nearby. And he wanted to spend more time with Evie.

"Do not decide this minute. You need to rest a few days. Then you may give me your answer," Henry told him.

"I will give it careful thought," William told him.

"That is all I ask." Henry clapped him on the back again. "We had best be heading back. The girls will be wondering what has happened to us."

Later that night William lay in his dark room. He listened to the wind howling outside. Thought of the fierce winter storms that rolled through the West Hampshire Colony.

Henry Mason makes a tempting offer, he told himself. This would be a good place to spend the winter. A place to rest before resuming the search for Catherine Hatchett.

If, indeed, he needed to search any further than this farm.

William could not shake the troubling feeling that Catherine lurked nearby.

He recognized her handiwork in the dying crops

and sickly animals. He sensed it in the fear on Henry Mason's face.

And in the eyes of Evie Mason's black cat.

Is that you, Catherine? he asked himself. Did you take the form of Evie's cat and bring your evil to this farm?

I have a responsibility to the Masons. To Evie. Did she not save me from the storm? From certain death?

When William thought of Evie, his heart raced. He had never felt this way before. Something stirred within him. Something wonderful he could not name.

"Do you want me to stay, Evie?" he whispered into the darkness. "Is that what I should do?"

William drifted off. Half asleep.

He thought he heard the door creak open.

Something clicked across the floor.

William opened his eyes.

Before he could sit up, the creature leaped onto William's face.

Thick fur covered his nose. His mouth. His eyes.

He could not see.

He could not breathe.

William gasped.

The fur filled his open mouth.

I—I can't breathe, he realized.

It's going to suffocate me!

## chapter 10

The black cat fur choked his throat.

William struggled to breathe. Felt his heart pound. Everything went bright red.

With a last burst of strength he reached up both hands. Grabbed the throbbing cat's body.

And pulled.

Yes! He lifted the cat of his face and heaved it onto its back on the bed.

With a furious hiss it squirmed under his grip. Tried to twist itself onto its feet.

William grabbed his knife from the chair beside the bed.

"Die, Catherine!" he cried. "Die at last!"

William thrust the knife downward. The tip of the blade gashed the cat's side.

The creature snarled in fury as bright red blood poured onto the black fur.

"Die!" William yelled, slashing the cat again.

The cat sunk its fangs deep into William's thumb, forcing him to cry out and loosen his grip.

The animal squirmed free and dropped to the floor.

William hurled his knife at the cat. The blade missed it by an inch and stuck in the floorboards.

The cat let out a howl of rage.

William dived for the knife. Yanked the blade free. Stared around wildly. "Where are you, Catherine?" he shouted breathlessly. "Where are you?"

He heard a soft scuffling sound outside the partially open door.

William lunged through the doorway, knife raised high in his hand.

Light blinded him.

A girl shrieked.

She will not escape me this time! William thought.

"What are you doing?" Evie Mason cried out.

She stood there in a white nightgown, an oil lamp in her hand.

Stunned, William backed away from Evie.

I could have killed her, he thought. He felt as though someone had punched him in the stomach. I could have killed Evie!

"What has happened?" Evie demanded. She took a step forward. Stared at the knife. It gleamed red with blood.

Jessica appeared behind Evie. A brown shawl draped over her head. Her face hidden in shadows.

William heard the sound of purring. Jessica cuddled the cat in her arms. She stared at him accusingly.

Evie turned to her cousin. "Raven!" Evie cried. "You are hurt!"

Evie gently examined the animal's fur. She raised her hand. Blood stained her fingers.

"What have you done?" she whispered. "What have you done to my Raven?"

"It is not a cat!" William managed to choke out.

Terror filled Evie's eyes.

William moved toward the cousins. "It is not a cat. It is Catherine!"

"Stay back!" Evie ordered, raising her hand. Her eyes fixed on the bloody knife in his grip.

"You do not understand." William let go of the knife. It clattered to the floor.

"That is not a cat. It is an evil girl. A girl named Catherine. She can take any form she chooses. I have hunted her clear across the colony. She is the one who brought you this bad luck."

"No! You are *mad!"* Evie exclaimed. "It is my cat. My poor, dear Raven."

"What is happening here?" a voice boomed. Henry Mason pushed past the girls.

"The creature." William pointed to the cat in Jessica's arms. "She attacked me."

"He tried to kill my Raven!" Evie told her father.

Henry took the lamp from his daughter and held her in his arms, soothing her. He glanced over at William. Shook his head in dismay. "You tried to kill our cat? Why would you do such a thing?"

"This is not a cat. It is a girl named Catherine Hatchett. A girl with a red crescent birthmark on her forehead. The mark is a sign of her evil nature. She brought you the same bad luck she gave our village."

William forced his voice to stay low and calm. "When we tried to hang her, she changed her form and escaped. I have been hunting her to put an end to her evil magic."

Henry held the lamp a bit higher. He gazed into William's eyes.

"You really believe this?" he asked slowly.

"I have seen her. I have felt her dark power. She killed my brother. And my father."

Jessica Mason moved into the light. She pulled the shawl down so it covered part of her face.

"He . . . he is insane!" she stammered. "He is a madman!"

William heard her voice for the first time. It sent a chill through him.

"He talks of evil power," she continued. "But he is the one bringing death into this house!"

"He is correct about our luck, though," Henry replied. "It is not only our farm. The whole area is suffering. The villagers claim it is the work of a curse."

"It is Catherine!" William insisted.

"You are certain of it?"

William nodded.

"And our luck . . ."

"It will change," William promised. "As soon as Catherine is dead, your bad luck will end."

He turned to Evie. Her eyes welled with tears as she stared at her cat.

"That is not Raven," he told her, his voice gentle. "Please believe me."

She shook her head. "I have had Raven since she was a kitten. She could not be evil."

William held his hand toward the animal. It purred contentedly as Jessica stroked its fur.

"I have watched Catherine turn into a rat, a horse, and a snake. She was in her cat form when I tracked her here. She must have come upon Raven and taken her place."

Evie's lips quivered. "Do you mean . . . ?"

He shook his head sadly. "I am sorry, but it is true. She killed Raven and found shelter with your family."

"How do you know this?" Jessica challenged. "What proof do you have?"

"I saw it in the cat's eyes," William explained. He turned to Henry. "You must believe me. We have to put an end to her once and for all."

"You tried to kill Raven," Jessica said bitterly. "And now you make up stories to excuse your crime."

Raven hissed at William. The cat twisted in Jessica's arms and sprang to the floor. Then it ran off down the hall.

"Let us go, Evie." Jessica took her cousin's arm and led her away.

The dark-haired girl turned back for a moment and stared at William.

Something cold glittered in her eyes.

Something familiar.

# chapter 11

William awoke to a bright blue sky, shimmering with sunlight. As he entered the kitchen, he worried about how Evie would treat him. What would she say?

To his relief, Evie greeted him warmly and smiled as she served him breakfast. William knew she did not believe her cat to be evil.

But he guessed that she understood his actions, and she had forgiven him for trying to kill her pet.

William glanced over at Jessica. Her cap covered much of her face. Although she did not speak, he sensed she had forgiven him, too.

She certainly is shy, he told himself. That shawl she wore last night covered almost as much of her face as the bonnet does.

During the meal, William found himself wondering about the cat. About Catherine.

Did I jump to the wrong conclusion? he asked himself. I was half asleep when Raven entered the room. Could my dreams have combined with the actual events?

Or did Catherine truly lurk nearby? Waiting for another chance to attack him?

Forget about Catherine for now, he told himself. You have been welcomed into the home of such a friendly family. Into Evie Mason's home. Forget everything else. Everything but Evie. He could not take his eyes off her as she went about her chores.

"Feel strong enough to do some chopping?" a voice boomed, interrupting his thoughts.

He turned to Henry, who stood in the doorway with an ax in his hand.

"The woodpile," Henry continued. "I am sure Evie could use some more kindling for that stove."

William felt his face flush. Had Henry caught him staring at Evie?

Nodding, he rose and accompanied Henry outside. The snow had melted. Birds flocked in the field.

"Those are the first birds I have spotted in a month," Henry commented.

The farmer picked up a heavy log and placed it on the chopping block. He smiled at William. "If there really evil at work, you must have scared it off last night. Our luck may have finally turned."

William certainly believed *his* luck had changed. He felt truly alive today.

For an instant he felt guilty. Joseph and Edmund Parker were dead. And so many others.

His brother, Joseph, would never feel the sun on his face again. Or hear a bird. Or kiss a girl.

Cataluna had ripped these things away from him.

It is all right to feel good, he told himself. Joseph would want me to feel good.

"I will chop first," Henry told him.

He hefted the big ax and swung it, testing its weight.

"You had best stand back," he warned.

William moved to the side. He marveled at how Henry Mason worked the ax. His movements appeared effortless. Yet he could split even the thickest logs in a single blow.

"Feels good to split a log in two," the farmer commented. "Very satisfying." He nodded for William to set another log on the block.

William stood the log on end and stepped back.

Henry swung the ax, bringing it down full force. The log burst in two. He placed one of the halves back on the block and quartered it. As he positioned the other half, he said, "Charlie could swing an ax like no one else."

"How did he die?" William asked.

Henry rested the head of the ax on the chopping block. "The strangest thing. He woke up with his stomach hurting. Said he felt very thirsty and went out to the well. That is where I found him."

He gestured toward the stone well at the far end of the house.

"He fell into the well?"

"No," Henry replied. "I found him lying beside it. Had the bucket next to him. No water in it."

"I guess he never got that drink," William commented.

"No, he drank. I found the cup in his hand. But the bucket did not contain water. It overflowed with blood."

William cringed. "Blood? The entire well is filled with blood?"

Henry shook his head. "No, I checked it. Fresh water, all right. But we have not drunk from it since. We have been using the rain barrel."

Henry stood back from the chopping block and swung. The log split apart. The halves flew in opposite directions.

"Yes, it feels good to swing an ax."

Henry positioned the next log himself, then handed the ax to William. "Here, you give it a try."

William stepped up to the block, planted his feet, and swung. The blade struck near the edge of the log and stuck fast. He had to pry it free.

William flushed. He did not want Henry to think he could not handle an ax. The next swing landed dead center, splitting the log.

"Now you have it!" Henry called.

William split a second log. A third. With each blow he felt himself growing stronger. More sure of himself.

Yes, it does feel good, he thought.

With Henry placing the logs for him, he made quick work of a half dozen of them.

Show him you can go faster! he told himself.

Gripping the handle, he worked with a smooth, steady motion. Log after log burst in two. The halves popped off the chopping block and landed several feet away.

Beads of sweat broke out on William's forehead. The head of the ax whistled through the air. He was really enjoying the *thunk* of blade striking wood.

William picked up the pace. So did Henry. As soon as William split a log, Henry had another in place. He would step back quickly and nod, and William would let the ax fly.

Show him how fast you can go! he challenged himself.

He grunted with each stroke of the ax. His breathing grew ragged. His heart raced.

Faster! he urged himself. I can go faster!

"Yes, faster!" he shouted.

"Whoa, young man!" Henry called out as he hurried to set another log in place. "This is not a race."

Henry chuckled again. His laughter sounded different to William. Softer. Almost feminine.

William swung the ax fiercely.

The laughter grew louder. Wild, feminine laughter.

The laughter of a girl.

"Catherine!" William cried in horror.

He tried to stop the swing in midair. But a power had seized his arms.

He slammed the ax down on Henry's wrist.
Henry's eyes went wide as the blade cut into him.
Sliced through flesh and muscle and bone.
Warm, wet blood sprayed over William's face.
Henry uttered a high, long wail of pain.
His right hand fell to the ground with a *thump.*

# chapter

# 12

Blood pumped from Henry's open wrist. Spraying the pile of logs. Drenching the ax and the chopping block.

William's stomach heaved. A sour taste stung the back of his throat. He stared down in horror at the hand lying on the ground.

From somewhere nearby, Catherine's laughter filled the air. Taunting him. Torturing him.

William raised his hands to his ears. But he couldn't shut out the horrible laughter.

I must help Henry! he told himself. I must! William turned and reached out both hands to the farmer.

"No!" Henry screamed. "Do not touch me!" He staggered to his feet. Clutched his blood-soaked stump with his left hand. His eyes searched wildly for something to stop the bleeding.

Jessica and Evie burst out of the farmhouse. "Noooo!" Evie uttered a long wail of horror.

Henry stumbled toward the barn. His knees wobbled as he snatched a length of leather harness and wrapped it around his forearm. Jerked it tight. Cutting off the flow of blood.

He fell against the barn wall, his face white as the snow around him.

Evie raced to her father. She eased him to the ground and cradled him in her arms.

"Monster!" Jessica cried. She flung herself at William. Pounding him with her fists. Biting and scratching.

Still in shock, William did not shield himself from her attack.

"Monster! You murdering monster! I will see you dead!" Jessica raged.

Finally William grabbed Jessica's wrists. "Stop," he ordered. "Stop now." He gave her a quick shake and then released her.

He turned to Evie and saw hatred and despair in her eyes.

"It . . . it was not me. . . ." he stammered, holding out his hand. Pleading for her to understand. To forgive. "It was her. It was—"

"Catherine?" Jessica cried, stepping between William and her cousin. "An evil girl named Catherine? *You* are the evil, William Parker! And you will be hanged! The village will hunt you down and hang you for what you have done here today!"

She turned to Evie. "Stay with Uncle Henry. I will get help from the village."

She ran toward the horse.

William slowly approached Evie. He reached out for her.

"Stay away from me, William," she sobbed.

William dropped his gaze to Henry. The poor man had lost consciousness. But his chest rose and fell steadily. The leather tourniquet had stopped the bleeding.

"Leave here!" Evie ordered in a trembling voice. "You have brought us nothing but pain. I cannot bear to see you." She buried her face against her father's chest.

William stumbled backward. Tears stung his eyes as he stared down at Evie and her father. He tried to speak. To explain. But he knew that no words could ease her pain.

He knew with all certainty that Catherine still lived. Still walked the earth, filling it with her evil.

He gazed a final time at Evie.

He could endure it no longer. He turned and ran.

Across the yard and through the field of withered corn. Into the woods beyond.

Branches slashed across William's face.

Catherine's cruel laughter rang in his ears.

"I will not hang, Catherine!" he screamed. "Nothing will stop me from destroying you!"

William pushed himself to run faster. Harder.

I must hide, he told himself. But where? Where?

William splashed through a shallow creek. He slipped on a mossy rock and crashed to his knees.

A dog howled in the distance.

William heard a musket shot.

They are after me already, he thought. He forced himself to his feet.

"I will find the monster!" a man shouted, his voice harsh with anger.

Close. Much too close.

Run, William urged himself. Run. You must survive. You must kill Catherine Hatchett. You must stop her evil. Do not let her beat you.

But two men stepped out to block his path.

"William Parker!" one of them shouted. "You cannot escape. You will hang from the tallest tree!"

# *part* 4

## *Shadyside*

## 1995

# chapter 13

Lauren shoved her algebra book into her backpack. She was heading to Marcy's to study with her. Marcy had read a horoscope that convinced her their math teacher would give a pop quiz the next day.

*And Marcy wonders why people hum the "Twilight Zone" theme music when she walks by!* Lauren thought. But Lauren didn't mind studying at Marcy's.

No Regina over there.

Lauren's stomach knotted every time she and Regina ended up in the same room. They hadn't had any more fights. Probably because Regina barely said a word to her. Or their parents.

Lauren grabbed her backpack. She hesitated. Then

picked up the car keys from her dresser. She ran her thumb over the mother-of-pearl circling the top of the ignition key.

Her fingers trembled. She tightened them into a fist. The sharp metal keys bit into her palm. "Don't freak out," she scolded herself.

Lauren hurried down the hall. She hesitated outside Regina's room. Sometimes she missed her sister.

They still lived in the same house. But it felt as though they lived on separate planets.

Lauren knocked lightly. No answer. She could hear music blasting through the door. Regina has the radio on so loud, she probably didn't hear me, Lauren thought.

Or maybe she's hoping I'll go away. Why risk it? Lauren asked herself. Regina's not making any effort to be friendly. Why should I?

Lauren started to leave. But she stopped when she heard the news come on Regina's radio:

"A hit-and-run driver killed a sixty-eight-year-old woman today on Division Street."

Lauren listened to the news story. The woman's car had been hit so hard that her head crashed into the windshield. She died instantly.

Lauren could imagine it all. The crash of metal against metal. The screech of tires. The sound of glass cracking.

And the blood. All the blood.

Lauren squeezed her eyes shut for a moment. Trying to force the gruesome picture from her mind.

"Mom, I'm leaving for Marcy's," Lauren called as she passed through the living room.

Mrs. Patterson sat on the couch reading. "Okay. Don't stay too late," her mother replied.

"I don't know, Mom," Lauren teased. "Sometimes I lose all track of time when I'm working on algebra problems. I start having so much fun that I forget to check the clock."

"I'm afraid you inherited your math skills from me," Mrs. Patterson said. "I still count on my fingers."

"Hey, good idea!" Lauren slammed out the door.

She trotted to the driveway, eager to get to Marcy's. Marcy always made her forget her problems. Or at least laugh at them a little.

The Cataluna stood waiting for her. Lauren circled in front of it. Her keys slipped out of her fingers. She bent down to retrieve them.

Something stained the bumper. A smear of red.

Oh, no, Regina, Lauren thought. What did you do?

She ran her finger over the long smudge. Paint. Metallic red paint.

Regina must have scraped a little paint off someone's car, Lauren thought. She smoothed her palm across the fender. No dent or anything.

But Regina is grounded, she remembered. So this means she started sneaking out again. Probably to meet Justin.

I'm not going to tell Mom or Dad about this, Lauren decided. I'm not listening to Regina call me a snitch again.

But I'm not covering for her this time. If Mom or Dad finds the mark—fine. Regina is on her own.

"Read me Regina's horoscope," Lauren asked Marcy. "I want to find out if there is a mental institution in her future."

Marcy scooped up an armful of magazines from the floor and tossed them on her bed. "Which one do you want to hear? This one is better for love. This one—"

"You pick," Lauren said. "You're the expert."

Marcy pawed through the pile. She threw the magazines she rejected back on the floor. "You don't really think Regina's crazy, do you?" Marcy asked, her dark brown eyes full of concern.

"No. Well, I hope not. But you should see her driving the Cataluna. Something happens to her. She changes when she's in that car." Lauren sighed. "Sometimes I wish our parents had never given it to us."

"Changes how?" Marcy asked.

Lauren tugged on her bangs. "I told you about that girl we almost hit. And Regina ran over a little boy's tricycle. She couldn't stop laughing."

"Sometimes I laugh when I get nervous. It almost hurts. But I can't stop," Marcy told her.

"That's different," Lauren insisted. "Regina laughed in a mean way. Really cold. As if she enjoyed scaring those kids to death."

Marcy stared at Lauren for a long moment. "Maybe Regina's been hanging around Justin too long," she finally suggested. "You know what a twisted sense of humor he has. Remember what he did with those frogs we had to dissect in biology class?"

"That was so gross," Lauren said.

Marcy yanked another magazine out of the pile. "This is the perfect one. Regina is a Sagittarius, right?"

Lauren nodded.

"Okay. We're going to solve this problem right now," Marcy declared.

"A boyfriend demands too much of your time," Marcy read. "Do an inventory check to decide if he's worthy. If not, wave goodbye. Remember to take your Flinstones vitamins this month. You need strength that only a little green Bamm Bamm can give."

Lauren grabbed the magazine from her friend. "So all I need to do is buy Regina some vitamins?" she joked.

Marcy yanked the magazine back. "No, genius. Regina needs to dump Justin. He's been suspended twice this year already. And last time he almost got Regina suspended, too. Justin's her problem. Not the car."

Maybe I should tell Marcy I've heard a strange voice in the car, Lauren thought.

No, that happened because I felt so worried about Regina. She spooked me by insisting she heard a girl's voice in the car. Spooked me so much I thought I heard it myself.

"Regina *has* gotten more impossible since she started going out with Justin," Lauren admitted slowly.

"The horoscopes are never wrong. Especially when they agree with me." Marcy grinned. "Tell her to wave goodbye to Justin."

Lauren reached into her backpack and pulled out her algebra book. "I hope your horoscope is wrong about tomorrow. Or I'm going to flunk that quiz."

Lauren rushed down Marcy's driveway. It was nearly midnight. I wonder if Mom will believe I couldn't tear myself away from the algebra, she thought.

She opened the car door and climbed inside. Then she slid the key into the ignition.

She stared at the wheel. Felt a cold chill.

Why do I suddenly feel so frightened?

You're scaring yourself, Lauren scolded. It's late. It's dark. And you're letting your imagination control you.

She checked the knob on the radio. The radio was definitely off.

No strange voices tonight.

Start the car, she ordered herself. Marcy is right. There is nothing wrong with the Cataluna. It hasn't been causing Regina to act so strangely.

Justin has.

He is always trying to find out how close he can get to the edge, Lauren thought. And he's pulling Regina along with him.

Lauren turned the key. The engine purred.

Less than a mile and you're home, Lauren told herself.

She pulled out onto the street.

As the car picked up speed, Lauren heard a faint rustling sound.

Then a *thud.*

What's that?

Lauren jerked her head toward the noise.

Her backpack had fallen off the seat.

Lauren laughed. I should have had Marcy read my horoscope, too! she thought. This month Pisces should beware of backpacks falling in the night.

Someone coughed.

A cold chill shot down Lauren's back.

No! Someone is back there, she realized.

Someone is hiding in the backseat.

# chapter 14

Is it just the voice I heard before?

Or is someone really back there?

Gripped with fear, Lauren slowly raised her eyes to the rearview mirror.

"Justin!" Lauren cried. "You idiot! What are you doing back there? You scared me to death!" She swerved to the curb and stopped.

Justin climbed into the front seat, grinning mischievously at her.

"What is your problem?" Lauren demanded. "I could have gotten into an accident. I could—"

"Whoa. Calm down, Lauren," Justin interrupted, placing a hand on her arm. "I'm sorry. I need to talk to you."

"You ever hear of a little thing called a telephone?" she snapped, still shaking all over.

Lauren clenched the wheel to steady her hands.

Justin saw how upset she was. "Sorry," he mumbled. "I didn't think it would scare you so much."

Lauren sighed. Typical Justin. "What did you want to talk to me about?"

"Regina," he answered. "I would have called, but I didn't want her to know."

Is he worried about Regina, too? Lauren wondered. Has he noticed how strange she's been acting?

"Something is wrong, isn't it?" Lauren asked, her voice tight with fear. "Is Regina okay?"

"You tell me," Justin replied. "I hardly see her."

He leaned closer to Lauren. "What do your parents have against me? They don't know anything about me."

Lauren studied Justin's face. His green eyes were intense, the muscles in his jaw tight. He cares about Regina, Lauren thought. He really does.

"I don't know what to tell you," Lauren said. "I guess they don't like the way Regina has been acting since you guys started going out. They think you're a bad influence or something."

Justin slid one arm around her. Lauren's stomach fluttered. She'd never been this close to Justin before. "Talk to your mom," he urged. "She'll listen to you, Lauren."

Lauren stared back at him. His face was inches from her own. She could feel his warm breath on her cheek.

"Tell her I'm not such a bad guy. I'm not a bad guy at all. Really."

Justin leaned closer. And kissed her.

A shiver raced down Lauren's body. She jerked away from Justin.

*"No, Lauren. Kiss him,"* a voice said.

Lauren blinked. She shook her head.

*"Kiss him, Lauren,"* the voice urged. *"Regina isn't here."*

"I want us to be friends, Lauren," Justin said softly.

"I . . . I shouldn't . . ."

*"Yes, you should, Lauren. It's what you want. Go ahead and kiss him,"* the girl's voice said, somewhere near Lauren's ear.

Lauren reached out and clasped her hands around Justin's neck. She pulled him to her and guided his lips to hers.

*"Yes, Lauren! That's the way, Lauren!"* the voice whispered.

She felt Justin's arms wrapping around her. Drawing her closer to him. Holding her tight.

*"He can be yours, Lauren. Don't let Regina have him."*

Regina. The name scratched at her brain.

But the sensation of Justin's lips on hers felt so good. So good.

*"Why should Regina have all the fun?"* whispered the voice.

"Regina!" Lauren exclaimed. She shoved Justin away.

Justin pulled her against him. "What's the matter, Lauren? Isn't that what you wanted?"

"Let go of me, Justin! Leave me alone!" she cried.

Justin grinned at her. "You liked it, Lauren. Don't pretend you didn't."

"Get out of here!" she demanded. "Get out of my car!"

"Lauren, we were just having a little fun. No big deal," Justin said, pretending to pout.

"You have a sick idea of fun. I want you out. Right now!" Lauren ordered.

He shrugged. Then he opened the door and climbed out.

"You really are a creep, Justin. How can you pretend to care about Regina?"

Justin laughed. "It was only a kiss, Lauren. And not too bad." He slammed the car door.

Lauren started the car and pulled back into the street.

How could I have done that to Regina? she asked herself. How?

Lauren's throat felt dry. Now it will be even worse between Regina and me, she thought. Even if Regina never finds out, I'll know. I'll know I betrayed my own sister.

Throaty, teasing laughter filled the car.

"No," Lauren whispered. "No. No. No."

The laugh grew louder.

"Who are you?" Lauren cried. "I don't understand what you want from me. What do you want from me?"

Lauren slammed her foot on the gas pedal.

I have to get away from that sound! she thought. Have to get away.

But the laughter swelled as she sped away.

Such cold, mocking laughter.

"Who *are* you?" Lauren shrieked, driving faster. Faster. "Who are you?"

*"Wouldn't you like to know?"* came the teasing reply.

# chapter 15

The next night Lauren opened Regina's door a few inches. She shoved a pint of Ben and Jerry's Chunky Monkey ice cream inside, waving it in the air.

If this doesn't get her, nothing will, Lauren thought. She heard footsteps pad in her direction. The door swung open.

Regina took the ice-cream carton from Lauren and walked to her bed. She pulled the top off the carton without speaking a word. Lauren pulled two spoons from her pocket and handed one to her stepsister.

Eight o'clock and Regina is already in her nightgown, Lauren thought. No makeup. Hair a total mess.

She's changed so much.

Lauren glanced at the TV on top of Regina's bookshelf. Regina had *The Wizard of Oz* in the VCR. Lauren knew Regina always watched that movie when she felt upset.

Lauren remembered watching the movie with Regina when they were little girls. "Regina, remember how I always hid my eyes when the Wicked Witch of the West appeared? I'd beg you to tell me when it was safe to uncover them."

"Yeah." Regina didn't smile.

Lauren sat next to her on the bed and scooped up some ice cream. They both stared at the TV.

"Regina, what's wrong? You're so different lately. Is it because you can't go out with Justin?"

Regina didn't reply.

"Because if Justin is the problem," Lauren continued softly, "I don't think he's worth feeling this miserable over."

"What do you know about it? Have you suddenly become an expert on guys?" Regina snapped.

"No," Lauren protested. "I'm worried about you, that's all."

"Worry about yourself, Lauren. You have a lot more problems than I do," Regina replied coldly.

"What does that mean?" Lauren cried.

"It means you are so messed up I can't stand to be around you." Regina threw her spoon on the floor. "You're the one who has changed."

Regina strode over to the door and yanked it open.

She stood there until Lauren left. Then Regina slammed the door closed.

Tears stung Lauren's eyes. Regina hates me, she thought. She really hates me.

She ran to her room and grabbed her purse. I need to get out of here for a while, she decided.

She found her mother and father watching the news on TV in the living room. "I'll be at Marcy's," she told them.

Mr. Patterson glanced up from the television. "You and Regina aren't fighting, are you? I thought I heard some yelling back there."

"Nothing serious," Lauren replied. She couldn't meet his eyes. "I'll be home early," she told her parents.

"Oh, Lauren," Mrs. Patterson called. Lauren stopped halfway out the door. "Be careful tonight. There's been another hit-and-run."

A knot formed in Lauren's stomach. "Another car got hit?"

Her mother shook her head. "No. A pedestrian this time. A man over in the Old Village. They think it may have been the same car."

"That's horrible!" Lauren exclaimed. "I promise I'll be extra careful."

She closed the door and hurried to the Cataluna. She couldn't help glancing at the bumper. "Oh, no!" A horrified gasp escaped her throat.

A dark red smear near one of the headlights.

Lauren touched it. Sticky.

She brought her fingers to her nose.
Not paint this time. Not paint. Not paint.
Lauren bent over and gagged.
Blood.
Blood on her fingers.
Blood on the Cataluna.

# chapter 16

Lauren gaped at the dark, damp smear on the bumper. She pressed a hand over her mouth, tried to stop her stomach from heaving.

Chills rolled down her body. She took a deep breath and held it.

Regina is the hit-and-run driver, Lauren realized. She stared at the blood on the bumper until it became a dark blur.

No. There must be another explanation, Lauren told herself. Regina could not be a killer.

But she's been acting so weird lately. She never talks to me. She's angry all the time.

And I know she's been sneaking out. Driving the car to meet Justin.

Once again she pictured Regina laughing after running over the tricycle. Regina had laughed and laughed. So heartless and cold.

She laughed after she almost ran down the little girl on skates, too, Lauren remembered. Sammy. How would Regina have felt if she had killed Sammy that day? Would she still have laughed?

Lauren hurried into the garage and grabbed an old T-shirt from the rag bag. She wet it in the sink.

Then she returned to the Cataluna and began wiping away the blood. Lauren watched the blood soak into the rag. Clean every inch, she instructed herself. If the police track down the car, it can't have one drop of blood on it.

She scrubbed the bumper until her hand ached. Sweat trickled down her forehead.

Lauren forgot how angry she felt at Regina. How much her sister had hurt her.

I have to protect Regina, she thought. I have to protect my sister.

When Lauren felt satisfied that no blood remained, she climbed into the car. She stuffed the bloody rag under her seat. Taking a long, deep breath, she pulled out of the driveway and onto Fear Street.

She didn't stop at Marcy's house. What could she tell Marcy? Not the truth. She couldn't ask her friend to protect Regina.

I have to deal with this alone, Lauren thought. It's the only way to save Regina.

I'll make sure Regina doesn't hurt anyone else, Lauren promised herself. I'll make sure she gets the help she needs.

Lauren drove down Park Drive. Past the hospital. Is the body of the man Regina killed lying in there somewhere? she wondered. Waiting for someone to claim it?

Lauren turned right on Division Street. The old woman died on this street, she thought. She tried not to picture the Cataluna crashing into the woman's car, sending the woman through her windshield.

At Mill Road Lauren turned right again. She didn't have a destination. She wanted to drive. To think. It didn't matter where.

Lauren reached the old, deserted mill. She parked the car facing the big paddle wheel and left the headlights on.

She grabbed the bloody T-shirt from the floor of the car. I have to hide this, somewhere where no one will find it.

She climbed out of the car. Left the door open.

Lauren's thoughts raced. This is crazy. This is wrong. But I have to protect Regina.

She climbed over to the old water wheel. It no longer turned, but a thin stream of water still poured down the stone chute.

Lauren knelt by the chute. The ground here was soft and muddy. She buried the bloodstained shirt in the mud. Shoved it deep into the mud and covered it. Then smoothed the mud over carefully.

For Regina, she thought. For Regina.

She shuddered. Turned to the stream and let the cold water run over her hands. It felt soothing. Helped to calm her.

When all the mud had been washed off, she stood up and started back to the car.

To her surprise, the high beams clicked on.

"Ohh!" A frightened cry escaped her throat.

The headlights flicked from high to low. High to low.

"Who's there?" Lauren called out in a trembling voice. "Who is it?"

In reply, the lights returned to their low setting and held steady.

Lauren moved out of the range of the headlights and approached cautiously. The door stood open. She could make out the front seats in the dim interior light.

Empty. No one inside.

"Is that you, Justin? Are you playing another sick joke?"

Silence.

"This isn't funny, Justin. It's you, isn't it?"

Silence.

She eased closer to the car. Peered into the backseat.

No one there.

She hopped in the driver's seat and reached for the key in the ignition. Before she turned it, the headlights flickered again.

Lauren let out her breath in a *whoosh*.

A short circuit, she told herself. That's all. It must be a short circuit.

Hoping that the ignition had not shorted, Lauren turned the key. The engine hummed. Yes! Lauren thought. After shifting into gear, she headed the car back to the road.

I've been acting like a crazy person, Lauren told herself. I haven't been thinking clearly at all. I've been in a panic, that's all.

Tomorrow I'll hardly be able to believe I thought Regina was the hit-and-run driver, she assured herself.

As she turned onto the road, something caught her eye in the rearview mirror. A flash of light. A pair of lights.

Lauren's breath caught in her throat.

The headlights of a car.

Someone is following me! Lauren realized.

Someone saw me bury the shirt.

But who?

## chapter 17

Lauren raced down Mill Road.

She kept her eyes on the rearview mirror. The headlights gleamed behind her.

That car is still following me, Lauren saw. Who is it? Who?

The police?

Could the police have identified the Cataluna? Did they know it had been driven in the hit-and-run accidents?

She struggled to see the car. But the lights flooded the mirror.

Could it be Justin?

Lauren made a sharp left onto Fear Street.

The other car turned, too. Kept close behind her.

Lauren took a deep breath and gave the Cataluna some gas. She sped toward the intersection up ahead.

At the last moment she slammed the brakes hard. Spun the steering wheel to the right. Shifted into third and hit the gas again.

Once she straightened out the car, she checked the rearview mirror.

Lost them!

Then she spotted two points of light behind her. Growing larger. Brighter. Closer.

Lauren slowed down as she approached the Hawthorne intersection. She flicked on the right-hand turn signal.

She started to turn. Then jerked the steering wheel and raced straight across the street.

At Canyon Road she spun the wheel to the left. The car skidded on two side wheels as she made the turn.

Breathing hard, her heart pounding, Lauren glanced over her shoulder. The other car was still there.

*Faster,* she urged herself. *Got to go faster.*

Lauren flew down Canyon Road. Parked cars became a blur on the left and right.

She stared into the rearview mirror. The headlights blinded her.

*The Old Village! I can lose them in the twisted streets of the Old Village!*

Lauren made another right. Entered the narrower streets of the old section of Shadyside.

The headlights of the pursuing car fell back.

Lauren turned left. Then right. She drove down Mission Street. Sped by the stores and offices of Division Street.

She pulled over to the curb and parked. Turned off her headlights. Waited.

She rubbed her fingers, trying to ease out the stiffness. She'd gripped the steering wheel so tightly, both hands ached and throbbed.

She waited a few minutes more.

"Lost them," she muttered. "I lost them."

Lauren turned the headlights back on and slowly pulled back out onto Division Street. She rolled down the window and took deep gulps of the cold air.

Her adrenaline rush faded. Her entire body began to tremble.

I have to talk to someone, she decided. Marcy. Marcy will help me figure everything out. Marcy is a real friend.

Lauren drove to Marcy's, careful to make lots of turns, careful to check the rearview mirror.

She parked in front of her friend's house, then trotted up to the front door. Her hand still ached. She knocked twice.

Marcy opened the door. "Lauren!" she gasped. "What's wrong? You look wrecked!"

She pulled Lauren inside. Then led the way down the hall to her room.

"Sit down," Marcy ordered. "I'm going to make us both some tea. Tea always helps calm you down. Then you're telling me everything." She hurried out of the room, closing the door behind her.

Lauren sat on the edge of Marcy's bed. She stared blankly at the wall. Her brain felt numb.

Marcy returned with two mugs of tea. She handed one to Lauren and sat down beside her.

"It's Regina," Lauren stated. She felt tears well up in her eyes.

"I don't want to believe it. I don't want to believe my sister is capable of murder. But I'm not sure. I'm not sure of anything. I feel like I'm going crazy."

"Oh, Lauren!" Marcy cried, wrapping an arm around Lauren's shoulders. "What has happened?"

Lauren gripped the steaming mug tightly. The warmth soothed her.

"I found blood on the Cataluna's bumper tonight," she said finally. Lauren took a long swallow of tea. "A few days ago I found paint on the Cataluna. Paint scraped off another car."

Marcy stood up. "Let's go look at the car," she urged. She pulled a flashlight out of her desk drawer.

Lauren shivered when she saw the Cataluna. But she followed Marcy across the lawn and over to the car.

Marcy leaned down and shone the flashlight onto the front bumper. Clean and shiny. Marcy glanced up at Lauren.

"I washed it," Lauren explained. "I didn't want the police to catch Regina. I don't want her to go to prison."

"But, Lauren," Marcy said, straightening up. "The bumper doesn't even have a dent on it. How could Regina have hit someone hard enough to kill them without leaving even a tiny dent? It's not possible."

"But the blood," Lauren insisted. "What about the blood?"

"Are you sure it was blood?" Marcy demanded. She ran her hands over the bumper again.

"I touched it," Lauren explained. "I smelled it. I'm sure it was blood."

Marcy slowly circled the Cataluna. Shining the flashlight over every inch. "No way this car was in two accidents. No way, Lauren. It's in perfect condition."

Lauren shook her head. "I don't know what to think. Regina has been acting so weird." She slammed her fist down on the hood. "It's this car!" she cried. "It's this horrible car. There's something wrong with it. It's evil. Evil!"

Lauren slammed her fist on the hood again.

Marcy grabbed Lauren's hand. "Stop it!" she yelled. "Stop it, Lauren!"

Lauren stared at Marcy. She's scared, Lauren realized. Scared that I'm totally losing it.

"You're not thinking clearly," Marcy said firmly. "You're letting your imagination run wild. Fighting with Regina has you completely messed up."

"Maybe you're right," Lauren admitted. "The car would *have* to be dented, wouldn't it?"

"Definitely," Marcy replied. "I think you need to go home and talk things out with Regina. I bet she has an explanation."

Lauren hugged Marcy. Then she climbed into the car. "Thanks, Marcy. Thanks a lot. Thanks for being such a good friend."

"Call me after you talk to Regina, okay?" Marcy turned and headed back to the house.

Lauren pulled away from the curb and started the car down the street.

She glanced in the rearview mirror. Darkness. No one following her.

Lauren concentrated hard on staying between the lines, using her turn signals, coming to a full stop. I feel as if I'm back in driver's ed class, she thought.

But the streets felt dangerous. Frightening. She kept expecting to see headlights following her—or a girl's voice laughing cruelly in her ear.

Lauren turned the corner onto Fear Street. Her parents had left the porch light on for her.

"I'm home," Lauren whispered. She parked in the driveway, leaped out of the car, and ran into the safety of the house.

Good, she thought, making her way down the back hall. Mom and Dad are already in bed. I'll be able to talk to Regina without worrying about them hearing.

Lauren crept down the hall. She stopped in front of Regina's door. Light under the door revealed that Regina was still awake. Music played softly on the radio.

"Regina," Lauren called. She rapped gently on the door. "I need to talk to you."

The light snapped off. The song on the radio cut off abruptly.

"Regina, I know you're in there. Open up. It's important."

Silence.

Lauren grabbed the doorknob. Regina will be furious if I barge in, Lauren thought. But too bad.

Lauren turned the knob. The door didn't open.

Regina had locked her door. She never did that.

"Regina!" Lauren cried. "Regina!"

"Lauren, is that you?" her mother called.

"Yes," she answered, sighing.

"It's late. Go to bed or you're never going to wake up in time for school."

"Okay, Mom," Lauren called back. "Sorry I woke you."

She stared at Regina's door, hoping Regina would change her mind. "You can't hide from me forever, Regina," Lauren murmured. She continued down the hall to her own room.

Lauren undressed and dropped into bed without brushing her teeth. She suddenly felt exhausted.

Almost immediately she fell into a deep sleep—and saw the white Cataluna in a dream.

The car was filled with blood. The thick red liquid seeped out the windows. Ran from the tailpipe. Dripped from under the hood.

With a cry, Lauren sat up and clicked on the light.

"That car is evil," she murmured out loud.

"Lauren, would you drive over to the dry cleaners and pick up my green dress?" her mother asked her two days later. "I want to wear it tomorrow and I'm right in the middle of making dinner."

"Maybe I'll ride my bike over," Lauren replied. "I could use some exercise."

Mrs. Patterson glanced at the clock. "You won't have enough time. It closes at six." She narrowed her eyes at Lauren. "Don't tell me you're tired of your new car already."

Lauren shook her head. "Of course not. I'll leave right now."

She didn't bother to remind her mother that it was Regina's turn to run errands. Lauren hated driving the car. But she couldn't stand the thought of Regina behind the wheel.

Okay, Lauren told herself. You are going to cross right in front of the car without checking the bumper.

Lauren had been checking the car every few hours. Even during the night. Making sure no blood had appeared.

She had tried to stop. But the car drew her to it.

She strode purposefully toward the car. Her eyes focussed on the house next door.

Lauren's footsteps slowed as she passed in front of the car.

Okay, you can take a quick peek, Lauren told herself. But that's it.

Lauren glanced down at the bumper.

Blood glistened on the shiny metal.

Lauren squeezed her eyes tightly shut. You imagined it, she told herself. You imagined it.

When I open my eyes, the blood will be gone.

Slowly, slowly, she opened her eyes.

# chapter 18

Lauren stared across the dinner table at Regina. Her sister had purplish circles under her eyes. She hadn't bothered to cover them with makeup.

*This ends tonight,* Lauren promised herself. *I have to make Regina tell me the truth.*

Lauren picked at her food. She dreaded confronting Regina.

She wanted to go straight to bed. Pull the covers over her head. And pretend that she'd never noticed anything strange about the car.

Or about Regina.

*But I can't,* she told herself. *Not after finding more blood on the Cataluna. If I don't stop Regina from killing again, then I am as guilty as she is.*

Guilty of murder. Guilty of murdering innocent people.

Regina asked to be excused. Lauren jumped up and followed her down the hall.

Lauren grabbed Regina's arm. "Let's go for a ride."

"No way," Regina replied coldly. "I'm not going anywhere with you."

"Yes, you are," Lauren insisted. Her fingers dug into Regina's arm.

"I know your secret, Regina. We can discuss it in the car. Or we can discuss it right here. With Mom and Dad."

Regina yanked Lauren's hand away. "Fine," she said, scowling. "But I'm driving."

"No—" Lauren started to protest.

"I'm driving or I'm not going at all. And you can tell Mom and Dad whatever you want." Regina stormed out the front door.

Lauren reluctantly followed. She needed to talk to Regina. She had to force Regina to confess to the killings. Once she did, they could decide what to do together to get Regina help.

But Regina always changes in that car, Lauren thought. What if she kills someone else?

What if she tries to kill *me?*

Regina climbed in the driver's side and slammed the door. She rolled down the window. "Well?" she called.

Lauren hesitated. Then she hurried around the car and slid into the passenger seat.

Regina turned the ignition key. Gunned the engine.

"Be careful," Lauren begged.

Regina didn't answer. She backed down the driveway, then raced down Fear Street.

Slow down, Lauren prayed. Slow down. Slow down. Slow down.

An intent stare on her face, Regina suddenly swerved hard to the right. The car bounced over the curb. Regina maneuvered the car onto the narrow bike path leading to Fear Lake.

"Hey—what are you doing?" Lauren cried. "Stop!"

Regina didn't reply.

The branches of the old trees seemed to reach out for her. They slashed and scraped against the windows of the car.

"Regina—are you crazy? Stop! What are you *doing?*" Lauren screamed.

Why is she driving us into the woods? Lauren wondered. Is she planning to hurt me? The trees thinned as they got closer to the lake.

No one will hear me if I scream for help.

Cold terror swept through Lauren's body.

"Stop! Please—stop!"

Regina slammed on the brakes. Lauren jumped out of the car.

Regina climbed out quickly and stalked over to Lauren. Anger contorted her features.

Lauren forced herself to meet Regina's stare. "I know your secret, Regina," she declared.

Regina laughed. A sharp, icy sound. "Okay, so you know my secret. So what?"

Lauren hadn't expected Regina to confess so quickly.

She doesn't even care that I know she's the hit-and-run killer, Lauren thought.

Is that because she plans to murder me, too?

"That's all you have to say? No explanations? No excuses?" Lauren cried. She stared at her sister. No guilt on her face. No sorrow. No fear.

Just cold anger.

"I don't owe you any explanations for sneaking over to Justin's," Regina said through gritted teeth. "Who do you think you are?"

"Nice try, Regina," Lauren replied. She forced her voice to remain calm and steady. "But we both know that's not your secret."

Lauren took a step closer to her sister. "I know you killed those people, Regina!"

"What?" Regina's eyes grew wide with surprise.

"Regina, I know you're the hit-and-run driver!"

"Lauren, are you *crazy?"* Regina shrieked. I'm not the hit-and-run killer! *You* are!"

# *part*
# 5

# *West Hampshire Colony*
# 1698

# chapter 19

William Parker fled from the villagers. He darted between trees and changed directions several times.

Finally he lost the two men who had discovered him. As he ran, he heard Catherine's evil laughter in his ears.

With a cry of despair he covered his ears. Forced himself to keep running.

It grew colder as the sun lowered, a winter storm in the air. He staggered through the fields, glancing back for signs of his pursuers.

He was growing tired. His legs ached. His head throbbed.

How would he survive the night?

William spied a shack up ahead. A small shelter used in the spring for boiling maple sap into syrup.

He stumbled to the shack and peered inside. Empty. Praise be, he thought, his heart pounding.

William crawled into the shelter and lay down on his back.

The roof had huge holes. Not much protection from the storm. But better than nothing.

William closed his eyes. He tried to forget what had happened, tried to shut the ugly pictures from his mind.

But he could not force them away. He saw Henry Mason sprawled on the ground. His hand lying in the dirt. His daughter cradling him in her arms. Evie's eyes filled with hatred.

No! He shook his head. Catherine is responsible, he told himself. Not I.

But am I not also to blame? he asked himself. A sick feeling clenched his stomach.

Why could I not forget this mad quest? I might have found a new life. A new home.

Instead, I chased Catherine here. I brought death and destruction to Henry Mason and his family. To Evie. To my dear Evie.

William crawled on his hands and knees to a stack of buckets used for gathering the maple sap. He huddled behind them.

As he gazed at the rough-hewn floor, he spied a spider crossing one of the planks.

"Is that you, Catherine?" he whispered.

She could be anywhere, he realized. Anywhere at all. Waiting to kill those William dared to care about.

William reached out and squashed the spider beneath his thumb.

What are you now, Catharine? A snake? A cat? A girl?

As if in reply, something rustled outside. He heard twigs snapping. Branches being pushed out of the way.

Someone—something—approached!

William crawled across the floor. He pressed his face against the wall and peered through a chink in the boards. He could not see anything in the dim light.

He heard voices shouting. Feet tramping through the underbrush. Several men calling to one another.

"Over here!"

"What is it? Do you see him?"

"A shed! Old Grady's maple shack!"

"Maybe he is hiding inside! We may still have our hanging tonight!"

"Go check it!"

Light glinted on a musket barrel as a man stepped into the clearing.

William jumped back from the wall. He searched wildly for somewhere to hide. A hole. Anything.

The stacks of wooden buckets surrounded him. Nothing more.

A board creaked beneath him. A loose floorboard! If he could pry it up, he might be able to squeeze underneath.

William dug his fingers under the edge of the board.

With a grunt, he jerked upward. The board creaked—then pulled free. He peered into the dark crawlspace below.

But before he could climb down, a dark figure leaped into the cabin.

And pointed a musket at William's heart.

# chapter 20

William stared into the musket barrel.

Waiting for the shot that would end his troubles. His quest. His pain.

His life.

Instead the barrel lowered. The door creaked closed.

Evie Mason rushed into his arms.

"William! I found you! Thank goodness you are well!"

"Evie!" he gasped, gazing in wonder into her soft blue eyes. "What are you—?"

"Shh!" She raised a finger to his lips. She rose and returned to the door. Then she cracked it open and stepped partway outside. "No one here!" she shouted to someone back at the trees.

William heard some answering voices. Then he heard footsteps heading away.

Evie hurried back to William's side.

"What are you doing here?" he asked in a whisper.

"I joined the hunting party. I had to find you. To make sure no one hurt you."

"But your father . . . I thought after what happened . . ."

She lowered her head. William could tell that she forced back tears. "It . . . it was so awful," she murmured. "Father lost so much blood. But we stopped it in time. He will live."

Evie raised her eyes to him. "I know that you are not responsible for injuring him. I . . . I believe you."

"You do?" he asked eagerly. "You believe that Catherine has brought her bad luck to your family?"

"I do now. After . . . after what I discovered."

She grew quiet. In the faint light of the shack he read the pain in her expression. He recognized something else, as well. Something new and troubling. "What happened?" he demanded. "Did you see her? Did you see Catherine?"

"It cannot be!" she sobbed, covering her eyes. "It cannot be true!"

"What is it?" he pleaded, holding her close.

"Remember what you told me? About the crescent-shaped birthmark on Catherine's forehead?"

He nodded.

"I saw it." Evie trembled. She stared down at the ground.

"Where did you see it?" he pressed. "You must confide in me."

"When my cousin Jessica was preparing to go to bed, I caught her removing her cap. The red crescent mark—it was on her forehead."

"Jessica?" His stomach tightened.

Somehow the news did not surprise him. Something in Jessica's voice had warned him. Something in her eyes.

"Jessica insists that *you* brought the evil, William. But our troubles started before you arrived. They started right after she came to live with us."

"You had never met her before, had you?" he asked.

She shook her head.

"I am afraid that this Jessica is not your cousin," he explained gently. "She is Catherine in disguise."

"What about my real cousin?"

William shook his head sadly. He did not want to admit the truth.

Catherine had most certainly found the real Jessica on her way to the farm. Then Catherine had killed her.

Catherine's powers allowed her to assume any form she wished. Even that of another person. Surely she had transformed herself into Jessica's double.

Evie seemed to understand and did not ask again.

"Does she know you discovered the crescent moon birthmark?" William asked.

"I do not think so. She had her back to me. I caught a glimpse of it in her hand mirror."

"Is she still at the farm?"

"Yes. Alone."

"And your father?"

"We brought him to the village. He can be cared for better there."

William nodded. "Then I must go back. I must finish this once and for all."

"Do you plan to kill Jessica?" Evie gasped.

William gripped her shoulders. "It is *not* Jessica," he said firmly. "It is *not* your cousin. The creature is not even human."

Tears ran down Evie's cheeks.

He hugged her. Felt her body shaking with emotion.

"I have to go back," he whispered. "It is the only way. This thing must be destroyed. Before it escapes and kills again."

"But what if you are wrong? What if it is really Jessica?" Evie demanded in a trembling voice.

He held her away from him and peered into her eyes. "Are you certain about the crescent moon, Evie? Did you see it clearly?"

"Yes. At her temple. It glowed red."

"Then it is Catherine. And she must be killed before she realizes she has been discovered."

Evie began to sob. "I cannot do this!" she wailed. "I cannot kill my own cousin. Even if she is *not* Jessica."

"You do not have to. You will wait here while I go back," William told her. "This is my quest. I will finish it. For my father and for my brother. For all those Catherine has destroyed."

Standing, he lifted her musket from the floor.

"Hurry back!" she called, reaching toward him. "Please. And be safe, William."

"I will hurry back to you as soon as I am able. I promise you." Returning to her side, he leaned down and kissed her. She threw her arms around him and held him close.

"The farm—is it far?" he asked.

"Only a few miles. Straight that way." She pointed toward the southwest.

"I will return for you. Do not worry."

He kissed her again, then hurried from the shack.

William Parker crept toward the Mason farmhouse. He sat for a few minutes at the edge of the forest and watched the house for any sign of activity.

No movement of any kind. Silence.

William crept out of the safety of the woods. Cautiously he approached the house. The musket was loaded and ready. He kept his long-bladed knife close at his side.

William reached the back wall. Circling the building, he peered through each window. He searched for any sign of Catherine.

Steam rose from a kettle hanging over the fire. Logs had recently been piled up.

She has to be here, he told himself. But in what form?

He glanced down at the ground. No snakes. No rats or mice. Not even a spider.

Approaching a bedroom window, he carefully

peered in—and saw someone lying on the bed, her back to the window.

He risked a longer peek and recognized Jessica. Was she asleep? He couldn't tell. Her cap shielded her face from view.

Not Jessica, he reminded himself. Catherine. Catherine of the Moon. Cataluna.

William eased open the back door of the house and slipped inside. He tiptoed silently across the kitchen and down the hall.

To the bedroom.

Jessica's door stood open. She seemed so peaceful as she lay there. Eyes closed. The brown cap pulled down on her forehead. Hands resting on the pillow.

So very peaceful.

Time to die, Catherine, William thought.

He moved closer. Stood beside the bed.

He raised the knife in both hands. Held the tip of the blade above Jessica's chest.

Could he do it?

Could he really kill her while she slept?

# *part* 6

# *Shadyside* 1995

# chapter 21

"Regina . . . *what* are you *saying?*" Lauren cried.

The woods suddenly turned darker, as if someone had turned off a light. A chill started at the back of Lauren's neck and ran down her spine.

"You heard me," Regina murmured, scowling. *"You* are the hit-and-run killer, Lauren. Don't try to switch the blame to me."

"You are so sick!" Lauren cried, raising her hands to her face. "How can you lie like that? Isn't it bad enough that you killed those people?"

"You killed them!" Regina insisted. "Face the truth, Lauren."

"But—but—but—" Lauren sputtered, unable to control her rage.

Regina held up her hand. "Stop. Just stop. I followed you in Mom's car. I know the truth."

"What!" Lauren screeched. "*You* were the one who followed me the other night?"

"I followed you more than once," Regina told her. "Do you want to know why? Because Darlene told me about you and Justin. She saw you and Justin parked in the car. Kissing. I couldn't believe it. I had to find out if my own sister had betrayed me."

"Regina, Justin and I—"

"That doesn't matter now," Regina interrupted. "What I found out when I followed you is so much worse." Regina's voice broke. "I saw you run down that man on Division Street. You aimed the car right at him. You murdered him, Lauren! And then you roared away."

Regina took a deep breath, then continued. "I followed you that night, too. The night you drove to the Old Mill to try and hide the evidence. You buried the blood-covered T-shirt to protect yourself, didn't you, Lauren?"

Regina blinked back tears. "That's why I've been locking myself in my room," she choked out. "I was terrified, Lauren. I didn't know how to confront you. I didn't know what to do. I was living with a killer. My own sister."

Regina turned away and started to sob. Her shoulders shook violently. She dropped to her knees on the ground.

Lauren suddenly felt shaky. She grabbed the hood of the car to keep from falling.

"No," she murmured. "Not me. Not me. Not me."

But ugly pictures began to form in her mind, pictures she had forced away. But now they returned, showing her the truth.

A man's face pressed against her windshield, face contorted in pain. Blood running from his mouth, smearing across the glass.

Metal slamming against metal. A scream of terror. Squealing tires. A body landing on the hood with a heavy *thunk*.

Her head thrown back against the seat. The seat belt jabbing into her stomach. The coppery taste of blood in her mouth as she bit her tongue. The bump as the tires rolled over a body.

A woman's face, twisted in agony.

And that voice. All the while, that laughing girl's voice, urging her on. *"Let's have some fun, Lauren. Faster! Faster! Faster!"*

"Noooo!" Lauren cried.

But now she knew that Regina had told her the truth.

I'm the hit-and-run killer, Lauren realized.

*"But you liked it, Lauren,"* the voice whispered in her ear.

She'd never felt so strong. So powerful.

Yes! I killed them! I killed them! Lauren realized.

*"You want to keep that power, don't you, Lauren?"* the voice demanded.

Lauren nodded her head.

*"You don't want Regina to steal it away from you,"* the voice teased.

Lauren shook her head back and forth. Back and forth.

*"It's not fair that Regina is so pretty. That she gets everything she wants. Is it?"*

"No," Lauren choked out. "No, no, no."

*"Then let's have some fun,"* the voice urged.

Lauren staggered to the car and lowered herself behind the wheel.

Regina remained crouched on the ground, her back turned.

Lauren turned the ignition key. The engine roared to life.

Regina jerked up her head and turned toward the car.

*"Kill her!"* the girl's voice instructed Lauren.

Lauren threw the car into gear.

*"Kill her now! Hurry, Lauren!"* the voice urged.

Lauren aimed the car at Regina.

Slammed on the gas pedal.

Shoved it all the way to the floor.

# chapter

# 22

The tires of the Cataluna spun in the dirt, sending up a curtain of dust. Then, with a hard burst, the car jolted down the bike path.

"Lauren—*no!*" Regina shrieked, raising both hands as if to shield herself.

The car bounced over the bumpy ground. The wheel spun crazily in Lauren's hands.

*"Kill her! Kill her!"* The voice rang out over the roar of the engine, the screech of the tires.

"Yeoww!" Lauren's head shot forward as the car lurched up. A hard bump.

Had she hit Regina?

No.

The car shot into the slender trunk of a pine,

cracking it, sending it toppling to the ground. It bounced off, jerking Lauren against the door. Hit another tree. Rocketed over a fallen log.

"Whooaaaa!" Lauren uttered a long wail. She slammed hard on the brake. But the car didn't respond. Didn't even slow.

*I'm heading right for the lake!*

Frantically she pumped the brake. Stomped on it. Stomped with all her strength.

The car shot forward.

"Stop! Please—why won't you stop?" Lauren cried.

The Cataluna bounced into the air—then flew over the marshy bank.

It made a loud slapping sound as it hit the surface of the water.

Lauren's chest slammed hard against the wheel. She uttered a gasp. Saw red. Struggled to breathe.

A cold spray of water splashed over her.

The car was sinking now. Sinking fast.

Murky cold water poured through the open windows.

Lauren grabbed the wheel. Tried to lift herself off the seat. Tried to pull herself . . . to free herself . . .

Going to drown. I'm going to drown unless I can get out. . . .

But her foot caught under the brake pedal.

She grabbed the door handle. Tugged to open the door.

But the door didn't budge.

Down, down. The cold water pouring over her, filling the car, filling it.

"No! Help! Help me!"

The car sank so quickly.

She choked as the icy water rose over her chin.

"Let me out! Let me—out!"

The water flowed higher, lifting her hair from her shoulders. Sealing her lips, her nose, her eyes.

Down, down.

Underwater now. Completely underwater.

And all the while the laughter in her ear, the cold, cruel, laughter.

Hands tugged at Lauren. Strong arms lifted her from the dark. A sound . . . a familiar voice . . .

"Lauren! Wake up, Lauren! Please—let her be all right!"

Other sounds. Sirens. Voices.

And glaring, flashing lights.

Someone rubbed Lauren's hand. She felt herself moving, floating. Being lifted away.

Was she floating? Was she flying?

Lauren fought the darkness. Forced open her eyes. Struggled against the blinding light.

"She's awake!" someone shouted. "She's alive!"

Lauren tried to speak, but her tongue would not move. Her lips quivered. Her whole body shook.

Cold. I'm so cold.

"Don't try to talk, Lauren. Everything's going to be all right." Regina's voice.

Lauren struggled to focus on her sister's face.

"D-did I hit you?" Lauren managed to stammer. "Did I—?"

"I rolled out of the way," Regina told her. "I'm okay."

Another voice broke in. "A little wet, though."

Lauren blinked rapidly. Her vision slowly cleared.

A man stood beside Regina, wearing the uniform of a firefighter. "She hauled you out of that car. All by herself."

"The car!" Lauren cried.

"They're pulling it out now," the firefighter told her.

"Noooo!" Lauren wailed.

"Rest easy now. We'll handle everything."

The firefighter motioned to some others. Lauren felt herself being lifted into the air. Placed onto a stretcher. The men carried her toward the flashing lights. Toward the ambulance.

Regina remained at her side. Clutching her hand.

"I . . . I'm sorry . . ." Lauren mumbled.

"I know," Regina told her.

"It wasn't me. It was the car."

"We'll talk about it later, Lauren. You rest now."

The stretcher slid into the back of the ambulance. Regina climbed in beside her.

Gazing through the open doors, Lauren saw the Cataluna. A tow truck pulled it up onto the shore, a long metal cable hooked to the white car's bumper.

The car stood there, water dripping from the fenders. Gleaming white. Sparkling.

*It's totally clean and undamaged,* Lauren saw. *Not a dent. Not a mark.*

One of the firefighters circled the Cataluna, then

approached the ambulance. He removed his hat and smiled at Lauren and Regina.

"I'd like to get a sports car like that." He shook his head. "It crashed into a couple trees before it hit the lake. But there's not a dent on it. Not even a scratch."

He started away, then glanced back at them.

"Man, that car is *wicked!*"

# *part* 7

# *West Hampshire Colony*
# 1698

# *chapter* 23

William Parker held the knife high over Jessica. He gazed down at her. His hand trembled.

Could he do it? Could he end Catherine's evil now with a single plunge of the knife?

She sighed in her sleep, stirred.

William took a deep breath—and slammed the knife deep into the sleeping girl's side.

Jessica's eyes flew open in shock. Her lips parted, as if to ask, "Why?"

Blood dribbled out of the corner of her mouth. Staining the white lace that framed her cap.

"Your evil shall no more walk upon this land!" William cried triumphantly.

Jessica tried to speak. But only a groan escaped her throat. She gazed beyond William. Into the distance.

Then her eyes closed.

She collapsed back onto the bed, and died.

"I have defeated you, Catherine Hatchett! This day I have avenged the deaths of my brother and father. And all the others you have destroyed. This day you are no more! This day belongs to me!"

Reaching down with a trembling hand, William yanked the bonnet off her head. Long black curls cascaded over her forehead. He pushed them away.

"What?" he gasped.

Where is the birthmark? Where is the red crescent moon?

William touched her forehead where the mark should be. And found not a crescent moon, but a small jagged scar.

"What magic is this?" he muttered, frantically rubbing the scar. Trying to make the crescent moon appear.

Laughter filled the bedroom, slicing through William like a blast of icy wind. Jerking himself upright, he spun around.

She stood in the doorway. Laughing with delight.

"Evie! What are you doing here?"

"Evie? You call me Evie? Why not use my real name?"

His eyes widened in shock. "Catherine . . ." he whispered.

"Cataluna, Cat of the Moon!" she declared, grinning with pleasure.

"But—"

"You were so easy to convince! So easy to fool!"

She touched a finger to her tongue, then rubbed at her forehead. The small red crescent moon appeared.

"Did you think I needed a bonnet? A little flour and water is sufficient to cover this mark!"

"But Evie? What about Evie?"

"Evie has been dead for weeks now. Since the day I arrived." Catherine shook her head gleefully.

William stared at her in horror. Slowly he began to understand how completely he had been tricked.

I have taken an innocent life, he realized. I have killed poor Jessica. More blood on my hands.

He thought of Evie and Henry and Jessica. Of his brother and father. Of the terrible evil that Cataluna had brought to this land.

With a shriek of rage he leaped at her. His fingers closed around her throat.

With a cry she toppled to the floor. He landed on top of her, his hands still around her throat.

Her eyes bulged. She struggled to breathe.

He tightened his grip. Felt her neck give in his hands.

William shook her. Shook her—until she disappeared.

"What?" William stared down at his locked hands.

Cautiously he opened them.

A tiny brown field mouse darted out and scampered down the hallway. Catherine had transformed again.

William scrambled to his feet and chased after the little creature. He stomped at it as it scurried out the back door.

As the field mouse scampered across the backyard, William snatched a shovel from against the house.

Desperately he swung the shovel. Again. Again. Trying to beat the mouse into the ground. To destroy Catherine forever.

At the edge of the trees William tripped and fell. His forehead struck the shovel handle, stunning him.

He shook his head to clear it. Rose up on one knee. Watched as the mouse became a sleek white horse and galloped into the woods.

He staggered after it. But it ran too swiftly. In seconds it left him far behind.

"I will find you!" he shouted, racing through the forest. Following her hoofprints in the soft earth, in the faint, fading light.

"I will find you, Catherine of the Moon! And the evil you have brought to others will be the evil that destroys you!"

The woods stood dark and silent. Yet something glowed in the distance.

A campfire? William thought. But no, it burned without flickering. As steady as the moon.

Approaching cautiously, he found not one light but two. Two beams of light that shone through the trees.

He moved to his left. Out of the path of the beams. And continued forward, toward the strange, unearthly lights. Lights that seemed to rumble.

He saw her then. In front of the light beams. No longer a horse or a cat or a mouse, or even the girl named Evie.

Catherine Hatchett. Standing motionless in the harsh glare of the lights. Staring into them, transfixed.

As William circled closer, he could make out Catherine's features. The crescent moon on her forehead. Her mouth hung open, her eyes wide. She appeared frightened as she gazed into the beams.

He heard the voice then. Not Catherine's voice. But a familiar voice, just the same.

"Do not be afraid, my daughter. I have come to help you." The voice of an old woman. The one named Crazy Gwendolyn who used to live in the forest near their village. William remembered her well.

"Do not be afraid, my daughter. This machine is from another place. Another time. Far, far away."

As William edged closer, a strange creature came into view. As big as a large wagon. Hard and shiny, as if carved from smooth white stone and coated with polish.

A dragon? he wondered. He recalled drawings he had seen of creatures from ancient times.

Perhaps the beams of light were flames shooting forth from the white dragon's eyes. Soft red lights glowed at its tail, he saw.

It hummed and rumbled with a throaty purr. A great beast waiting to attack.

"I was born not in the past but the future," the voice of Gwendolyn continued from deep within the creature. "When I discovered I was with child, I used this machine to travel three hundred years into the past. To escape from a man who would have hurt you,

Catherine. Now your life is yet again in danger. And once more this machine will save you, my child."

William edged closer. He knelt beside one of the rear red lights.

"Do not be afraid, my Catherine. Climb in, and I will take you away. They will never find you. They will not be able to hunt you down."

William crouched lower as Catherine moved to the other side of the white dragon. Metal rasped against metal, like a musket being cocked. Then Catherine disappeared inside. Devoured by the very creature that called itself her mother.

Another clash of metal. This time a door being slammed.

The rumbling grew louder. The dragon rattled and shook.

"I will take you away to the future!" Catherine's mother declared as the sound grew deafening. "They will never hurt you again!"

She is going to escape! William realized. I cannot let her get away!

He dived at the creature. Leaped through the air. Through an opening in the side of the dragon. Plunged inside the rumbling beast.

The dragon shouted. It roared.

And burst into flames.

# chapter 24

William Parker's skin sizzled. Great sheets of flame shot up all around him, filling the belly of the dragon with an eerie light.

He could see Catherine in front of him, low in some sort of chair. Her hands rested on a white wheel. Her head was thrown back as she laughed with delight.

Blistering heat filled the insides of the creature. Fire seemed to pour from his arms and legs, from Catherine's hair and head and body—out of the depths of the creature itself.

William screamed, but he could not even hear himself above the roar of the flames.

He struggled to move. To get away. To escape the horrible heat.

But a blast of burning air held him down, trapped him inside the beast.

In his terror he tried to think clearly. Calmly.

What kind of monster is this? he wondered, forcing himself to gaze around.

It resembled a carriage. The most unusual carriage he had ever seen. With seats and pedals and a panel of lights and dials. But without whip or reins. And with no team of horses in harness.

William worked up his courage and peered out the window at his side. The dragon flew forward. Racing down a strange-looking roadway. A road not of dirt, but of the smoothest unbroken stone. With curious white lines—solid and broken—down the center.

Through the flames William gazed upon incredible wonders. Great buildings of brick and metal. Dozens of dragons—blue, green, red, silver, white. Lights everywhere!

William hunched down on the back floor. He clutched the seats as the creature flew ever faster down the road.

The creature roared and hummed, weaving back and forth.

William flew back against the seat. He spied Catherine's face in a mirror suspended in front of her. Saw her eyes on him. Saw the glint of surprise in them.

Through the wide glass in front of her, another dragon loomed ever closer. Blue and low.

They raced toward the blue dragon. People sat trapped inside its belly. Terror on their faces.

He shuddered as the dragons roared. Then a terrible screeching. Metal crashed and crumpled as they rammed into each other.

Devouring the people inside.

William fell onto the floor. The world spun around him. Exploded into a white-hot ball of fire.

His body burst with pain. Crushing pain.

"Catherine!" he murmured.

Then the dark silence swallowed him.

"The convertible is totaled. And this baby doesn't have a scratch. Unbelievable." Joe Henderson glanced over at his partner.

"Yeah," Shelly Kline agreed, pushing back her blue hat. She circled the white sports car. "And it must have been doing a hundred when they crashed."

Kline sighed. "I hate the thought of calling those kids' parents. Did you notice the out-of-state plates? I bet it's one of the first times these kids got permission to go on a trip by themselves."

"Any of them going to make it?" her partner asked.

"The medics are working on a couple, but I doubt it."

Henderson stared through the unbroken windshield of the white sports car. Studied the teenage boy and girl inside, the girl in front, the boy crushed in the back. "I wonder where these two were headed. A costume party, you think?"

Kline nodded. "Or maybe a school play. Those clothes are colonial-looking."

One of the medics headed in their direction.

"No hurry for these two. They're both already dead."

# epilogue

The officer was wrong. There were survivors in the white car.

Catherine Hatchett survived.

Her mother's strange machine brought her three hundred years into the future. It crushed her body, but it left her spirit alive.

Alive to inhabit that monster. A ghost in the machine. A spirit inside the sports car known as *Cataluna.*

Her evil became the car's evil. Her voice its deadly music. Her laughter its hideous cry.

And what of William Parker? What of *my* spirit?

I, too, survived.

I refused to let death cheat me. I refused to give up my struggle against Catherine of the Moon.

For I had made a vow that I would hunt her down.

And I would have my revenge.

Yes, my chase continued. Across colonies and centuries.

To this strange place three centuries from when I first lived.

To a town called Shadyside.

And a street named Fear Street.

Ah, but that is a story for another place.

Another time.

## *About the Author*

"Where do you get your ideas?"

That's the question that R. L. Stine is asked most often. "I don't know where my ideas come from," he says. "But I do know that I have a lot more scary stories in my mind that I can't wait to write."

So far, he has written more than fifty mysteries and thrillers for young people, all of them bestsellers.

Bob grew up in Columbus, Ohio. Today he lives in an apartment near Central Park in New York City with his wife, Jane, and fourteen-year-old son, Matt.

THE NIGHTMARES
NEVER END . . .
WHEN YOU VISIT

Next . . .

## THE CATALUNA CHRONICLES
## BOOK #3: *THE DEADLY FIRE*

They came from different centuries. Different worlds. But the same evil force could destroy both their lives.

In 1698 a girl called Bad Luck Catherine killed William Parker's brother. William swore revenge. His quest led him three hundred years into the future—to a place called Shadyside.

In 1995 a car called the Cataluna killed Buddy McCloy's brother. Buddy wants to destroy the car. But he is strangely drawn to it—drawn to the spirit of Bad Luck Catherine trapped inside the car.

In one night, the fate of William, Buddy, and Catherine will be decided. The night of a drag race. A race to the death.

R·L·STINE

presents

THE

FEAR STREET®

1996 CALENDAR

Spend 1996 on

FEAR STREET

Vampires, evil cheerleaders, ghosts, and all the boys and ghouls of R. L. Stine's Fear Street books are here to help you shriek through the seasons. It's the perfect way to keep track of your days, nights, and nightmares....

Special Bonus Poster

A map of Shadyside showing where all the horrors of Fear Street happened. Take a terrifying tour of the spots where your favorite characters lived—and died.

Coming soon

1098

A Fear Street Calendar/Published by Archway Paperbacks

# L.J. SMITH

# THE FORBIDDEN GAME TRILOGY

**A boardgame turns dangerous when the teenage players are trapped inside and stalked by a bizarre supernatural force.**

---

**VOLUME I: THE HUNTER** ......87451-9/$3.99
If he wins, she's his forever more....

**VOLUME II: THE CHASE** .......87452-7/$3.50
He's back - and coming to claim her at last!

**VOLUME III: THE KILL** ..........87453-5/$3.99
Step into the Devil's playground....

---

And Look for the L.J. Smith Trilogy...

**DARK VISIONS, Vol. I: The Strange Power**
................87454-3/$3.50

**DARK VISIONS, Vol. II: The Possessed**
................87455-1/$3.50

**DARK VISIONS, Vol. III: The Passion**
................87456-X/$3.50

All Available from ArchwayPaperbacks
Published by Pocket Books

**Simon & Schuster Mail Order**
**200 Old Tappan Rd., Old Tappan, N.J. 07675**

Please send me the books I have checked above. I am enclosing $_____(please add $0.75 to cover the postage and handling for each order. Please add appropriate sales tax). Send check or money order–no cash or C.O.D.'s please. Allow up to six weeks for delivery. For purchase over $10.00 you may use VISA: card number, expiration date and customer signature must be included.

Name ____________________

Address ____________________

City ____________________ State/Zip __________

VISA Card # ____________________ Exp.Date __________

Signature ____________________

964-09

# RICHIE TANKERSLEY CUSICK

- ☐ *VAMPIRE*..................70956-9/$3.99
  *It's the kiss of death...*
- ☐ *FATAL SECRETS*..................70957-7/$3.99
  *Was it an accident--or was it cold-blooded murder?*
- ☐ *BUFFY, THE VAMPIRE SLAYER*..................79220-2/$3.99
  *(Based on the screenplay by Joss Whedon)*
- ☐ *THE MALL*..................70958-5/$3.99
  *Someone is shopping for murder!*
- ☐ *SILENT STALKER*..................79402-7/$3.99
  *Terror is her constant companion as death waits in the wings...*
- ☐ *HELP WANTED*..................79403-5/$3.99
  *The job promised easy money -- but delivered sudden death!*
- ☐ *THE LOCKER*..................79404-3/$3.99
  *Is someone reaching for help--from the grave?*
- ☐ *THE DRIFTER*..................88741-6/$3.99
- ☐ *SOMEONE AT THE DOOR*..................88742-4/$3.99
- ☐ *OVERDUE*..................88743-2/$3.99

**Available from Archway Paperbacks**

Simon & Schuster Mail Order
200 Old Tappan Rd., Old Tappan, N.J. 07675
Please send me the books I have checked above. I am enclosing $_____(please add $0.75 to cover the postage and handing for each order. Please add appropriate sales tax). Send check or money order--no cash or C.O.D.'s please. Allow up to six weeks for delivery. For purchase over $10.00 you may use VISA: card number, expiration date and customer signature must be included.

Name ____________________

Address ____________________

City ____________________ State/Zip ____________

VISA Card # ____________________ Exp.Date ____________

Signature ____________________ 733-08